POIL DE CAROTTE

JULES RENARD
POIL DE CAROTTE

With the original illustrations by
FÉLIX VALLOTTON

Translated from the French by
RALPH MANHEIM

A NONPAREIL BOOK

DAVID R. GODINE · PUBLISHER

BOSTON

This is a Nonpareil Book
published in 2015 by
DAVID R. GODINE · *Publisher*
Post Office Box 450
Jaffrey, New Hampshire 03452
www.godine.com

Translation Copyright © Walker and Company 1967
This reprint of *Poil de Carotte*, is published by
David R. Godine, Publisher, Inc.
by arrangement with Bloomsbury Publishing Inc.

LIBRARY OF CONGRESS CATALOGING-IN-PUBLICATION DATA

Renard, Jules, 1864–1910, author.
[Poil de Carotte. English]
Poil de Carotte / Jules Renard ; Translated from the French by
Ralph Manheim ; Illustrations by Félix Vallotton.
pages   cm
Summary: Neglected by his parents, bullied by his peers, left to
wander the streets and woods by himself (that is, when he isn't locked
in his room or the cellar for punishment), the little redheaded boy
known as "Poil de Carotte" ["Carrot Top"] manages to survive
the worst that rural France has to offer.
ISBN 978-1-56792-523-4 (alk. paper)
1. Renard, Jules, 1864–1910—Translations into English.
I. Manheim, Ralph, 1907–1992, translator.
II. Vallotton, Félix, 1865–1925, illustrator. III. Title.
PQ2635.E48A2413 2014
842'.912—dc23
2014035109

First Nonpareil Edition
Printed in the United States of America

CONTENTS

CONTENTS

CONTENTS

"Why do you call him Poil de Carotte? Because of his red hair?"

"His soul is even redder than hell-fire," says Madame Lepic.

THE HENHOUSE

I'LL BET Honorine has forgotten to close the henhouse," says Madame Lepic.

She's right. It can be seen from the window. Out there in the darkness at the far end of the yard, the open door of the little henhouse is a black square silhouetted against the sky.

"Felix, suppose you go close it?" says Madame Lepic to the eldest of her three children.

"I'm not here to look after the chickens," says Felix, a pale, indolent and cowardly boy.

"What about you, Ernestine?"

"Oh no, Mama, I'd be too scared."

Big brother Felix and sister Ernestine hardly raise their heads to answer. Their elbows on the table, their foreheads almost touching, they are enormously interested in their reading.

"How stupid of me," says Madame Lepic. "I'd forgotten all about him. Poil de Carotte, go close the henhouse."

She calls her last-born by this endearing nickname because he has red hair and freckles. Poil de Carotte, who is playing at nothing much under the table, stands up and says timidly:

"But, Mama, I'm afraid too."

"What's that?" says Madame Lepic. "A big boy like you. Don't make me laugh. Will you kindly get a move on."

"We know him," says his sister Ernestine. "He's as brave as a bull."

"He fears neither man nor beast," says Felix, his big brother.

Puffed up with pride at the compliments and shamed by his unworthiness, Poil de Carotte tries to fight down his fear. To encourage him once and for all, his mother promises him a box on the ear.

"Light the way for me at least," he says.

Madame Lepic shrugs her shoulders, Felix smiles contemptuously. Only Ernestine takes pity on him. She picks up a candle and accompanies her little brother to the end of the corridor.

"I'll wait here," she says.

But then her candle wavers and dies in a sudden gust of wind, and she runs away in terror.

Buttocks glued together, heels solidly planted, Poil de Carotte stands trembling in the darkness. The blackness is so dense that he thinks he's blind. From time to time a gust of wind enfolds him like an icy sheet and threatens to carry him away. It seems to him that foxes, or even wolves, are breathing on his fingers, on his cheeks. The only way is to make a blind dash, head down so as to bore through the blackness. He gropes, he finds the latch of the door. At the sound of his steps, the hens flutter and cluck in their roost. Poil de Carotte cries out, "Pipe down, will you, it's me," shuts the door and runs. Proud and panting, he returns to the warmth and light.

He feels as if he had exchanged his muddy, rain-soaked rags for a light new garment. He smiles, stands proudly erect, and waits for congratulations. Now that the danger is past, he studies their faces for a sign of the worry they've felt.

But big brother Felix and sister Ernestine go on quietly with their reading, and Madame Lepic says in her usual voice, "Well, Poil de Carotte, from now on you can close it every night."

THE PARTRIDGES

AS USUAL, Monsieur Lepic empties his game bag on the table. It contains two partridges. Big brother Felix marks them down on the slate that hangs on the wall. That is his chore. Each of the children has one. Sister Ernestine cleans and plucks the birds. As for Poil de Carotte, his special task is to finish off the wounded game, a privilege he owes to the well-known hardness and coldness of his heart.

The two partridges flail about and wriggle their necks.

MADAME LEPIC

Well, what are you waiting for?

POIL DE CAROTTE

Mama, I'd just as soon take a turn at marking them on the slate.

MADAME LEPIC

The slate is too high for you.

POIL DE CAROTTE

Then I'd just as soon pluck them.

MADAME LEPIC

That's no job for a man.

Poil de Carotte takes the two partridges. Obligingly the family gives him the usual instructions. "You know, you take them by the neck. Just push back the feathers and squeeze." Holding them behind his back, one in each hand, he starts in.

MONSIEUR LEPIC

Two at once, my word!

POIL DE CAROTTE

It's quicker that way.

MADAME LEPIC

Let's not be squeamish. You know you love it deep down.

The partridges struggle frantically. They flap their wings and send feathers flying. They simply refuse to die. He'd find it easier to strangle a friend. He wedges them between his knees to hold them still. Red and white by turns, bathed in sweat, head high to avoid seeing, he squeezes harder.

They keep on struggling. In a frenzy to get it over with, he takes them by the feet and dashes their heads against the tip of his shoe.

"Oh, the brute! The brute!" cry big brother Felix and sister Ernestine.

"He really is vicious," says Madame Lepic. "The poor things! I wouldn't want to be in their place, not in his clutches."

Monsieur Lepic is a hardened hunter, yet he leaves the room, sickened.

"There," says Poil de Carotte, throwing the dead partridges on the table.

Madame Lepic turns them over and over. Blood is flowing from their little smashed skulls. And a bit of brains.

"It was high time to take them away from him," she says. "What a mess!"

Big brother Felix says, "It's a fact he hasn't made a very good job of it this time."

C'EST LE CHIEN

IT WAS THE DOG

ELBOWS on the table, Monsieur Lepic and sister Ernestine are reading beneath the lamp, he his paper, she the book she has won as a prize at school; Madame Lepic is knitting, big brother Felix is toasting his feet by the fire, and Poil de Carotte on the floor is remembering things.

Suddenly Pyramus, who is asleep under the doormat, lets out a muffled growl.

"Sh-sh," says Monsieur Lepic.

"Idiot!" says Madame Lepic.

Suddenly Pyramus barks so violently that everyone starts. Madame Lepic clasps her hand to her heart. Monsieur Lepic clenches his teeth and gives the dog a disapproving look. Big brother Felix starts cursing, and soon the noise is deafening.

"Quiet, you cur. Pipe down."

Pyramus barks louder than ever. Madame Lepic whacks him, Monsieur Lepic hits him with his newspaper, then gives him a kick. Pyramus lies on his belly, muzzle lowered for fear of the blows, and howls. Furious, his muzzle colliding with the doormat, he seems to be ripping his voice to shreds.

The Lepics are beside themselves with rage. Menacing, they stand over the recumbent dog, who sticks to his guns. The windowpanes squeak, the stovepipe bleats, and even sister Ernestine is yelping.

But without waiting to be told, Poil de Carotte has gone out to see what's wrong. Maybe a farmhand who's been working late, going quietly home—unless he's climbing the garden wall to steal something.

Poil de Carotte makes his way down the long dark corridor, holding out his hands in the direction of the door. He finds the bolt and draws it with a crash, but he doesn't open the door.

In times gone by he had exposed himself to danger. He'd go outside and try to frighten the enemy by whistling, singing, and stamping his feet.

But now he cheats. His parents imagine him boldly searching every nook and cranny and making the circuit of the house like a faithful watchman. But nothing of the sort. He just stands motionless behind the door. Someday he'll be caught, but the trick has been working quite a while.

His only fear is that he may have to sneeze or cough. He holds his breath. If he raises his eyes to the little window over the door, he sees three or four stars whose glittering purity chills his blood.

But now it's time to go back in. It wouldn't do to stay too long. They might get suspicious.

With his frail little hands he shakes the heavy bolt again. It squeaks in its rusty clamps. Then he pushes it as noisily as he can to the end of the groove. The clatter will make them think that he has come a long way and done his duty. With a tingling in the small of his back, he hurries back to reassure the family.

Same as the last time, Pyramus has fallen silent during his absence. The Lepics have calmed down and resumed their invariable places. Though no one asks him anything, Poil de Carotte, who has got into the habit, announces: "It was only the dog dreaming."

LE CAUCHEMAR

THE NIGHTMARE

POIL DE CAROTTE doesn't like overnight guests. They upset his routine; they take his bed and oblige him to sleep with his mother. And though in the daytime he has every fault, his main fault at night is snoring. Of course he snores on purpose.

The big room, glacial even in August, has two beds in it. One is Monsieur Lepic's; Poil de Carotte will have to sleep in the other, on the wall side, next to his mother.

Before dropping off, he coughs a few times discreetly under the sheet to clear his throat. But maybe he snores through his nose. He blows gently through his nostrils to make sure they are not stopped up. He practices not breathing too hard.

But the moment he falls asleep, he starts snoring. It seems to be a passion with him.

Immediately Madame Lepic digs two fingernails into the fattest portion of one of his buttocks. That is her chosen weapon.

Poil de Carotte's scream wakes Monsieur Lepic, who inquires: "What's the matter?"

"He's had a nightmare," says Madame Lepic.

And softly, like an old nurse, she hums a lullaby. It sounds Indian.

Bracing his forehead and knees against the wall as though to demolish it, pressing his palms against his buttocks to parry the pinch which is the inevitable response to the first note of his guttural vibrations, Poil de Carotte falls back asleep in the big bed, on the wall side, next to his mother.

SAUF VOTRE RESPECT

BEGGING YOUR PARDON

IT GRIEVES ME to say this, but at an age when other boys take communion clean in body and soul, Poil de Carotte still soils himself. One night, for fear of asking, he waited too long.

He had hoped, by means of graduated wrigglings, to appease his distress. What optimism!

Another night he dreamed that he was leaning comfortably against a secluded boundary stone, and still innocently asleep, did it in his sheets. He wakes up.

No more boundary stone than bounds to his amazement.

Madame Lepic is careful to keep her temper. Calmly, indulgently, maternally, she cleans up. And next morning Poil de Carotte even gets his breakfast in bed like a spoiled child.

Yes, his soup is brought to him in bed, a carefully prepared soup in which Madame Lepic with a wooden spatula has dissolved a little of it, oh, very little.

At his bedside big brother Felix and sister Ernestine watch

Poil de Carotte slyly, ready to burst out laughing at the first sign. Spoonful by little spoonful, Madame Lepic feeds her child. She seems, out of the corner of her eye, to be saying to big brother Felix and sister Ernestine: Look sharp! This is too good to miss.

Yes, Mama.

They are already enjoying the grimaces to come. They ought to have asked a few of the neighbors in. Finally, with a last look at the older children as though to ask them: Are you ready?—Madame Lepic slowly, very slowly, lifts up the last spoonful, plunges it into Poil de Carotte's wide-open mouth, rams it deep down into his throat, and says with an air of mingled mockery and disgust:

"Ah, my little pig, you've eaten it, you've eaten it, your own from last night."

"I thought so," Poil de Carotte answers simply, without making the hoped-for face.

He's getting used to it, and once you get used to a thing, it ceases to be the least bit funny.

LE POT

THE CHAMBER POT

I

HAVING SUFFERED more than one accident in bed, Poil de Carotte is careful to take his precautions every evening. In the summer it's easy. At nine o'clock when Madame Lepic sends him to bed, he takes a little turn outside, and the night is uneventful.

In the winter his little stroll becomes a chore. At nightfall when he closes the henhouse, he takes a first precaution, but that can hardly be expected to carry him through till morning. They eat dinner, they sit around the table, the clock strikes nine. By now it has been night a long time, and this night will last forever. A second precaution is in order.

And as usual at this hour he questions himself:

"Do I need to? Or don't I need to?"

Ordinarily his answer is "yes," either because he frankly can't put it off or because the moonlight gives him courage. Sometimes Monsieur Lepic and big brother Felix set him an example. Besides, he doesn't always have to go far from the house, way out to the ditch beside the road, which is almost in the open country. Usually he stops at the foot of the stairs; it all depends.

But tonight the rain is needling the windowpanes, the wind has put out the stars, and the walnut trees are howling in the fields.

"Luckily," Poil de Carotte concludes after deliberating without haste, "I don't need to."

He says good night to all, lights a candle, and goes to his bare, solitary room at the end of the corridor on the right. He undresses, goes to bed, and awaits Madame Lepic's visit. With one stroke she tucks him in tight and blows out the candle. She leaves him the candle but no matches. And she locks the door because he is easily frightened. He likes to dream in the darkness. He reviews his day, congratulates himself on a number of narrow escapes, and anticipates equal luck for the next day. He feels confident that Madame Lepic will pay him no heed for two days running, and with this dream he tries to fall asleep.

No sooner has he closed his eyes than he becomes aware of a familiar feeling of distress. "It was bound to happen," he says to himself.

Anybody else would get up. But Poil de Carotte knows there is no chamber pot under the bed. Though Madame Lepic would swear it's not true, she always forgets to leave one. And anyway, what for, since Poil de Carotte always takes his precautions?

Instead of getting up, Poil de Carotte calculates. "Sooner

or later," he says to himself, "I'll have to give in. And the more I resist, the more I accumulate. But if I make pipi right away, there won't be very much and my sheets will have time to dry by the heat of my body. I know from experience that Mama won't see a thing."

Poil de Carotte relieves himself, closes his eyes again with a feeling of complete security, and falls into a sweet sleep.

II

Suddenly he wakes up and listens to his belly.

"Oh, oh!" he says. "Trouble."

He had thought it was all taken care of. No such luck. At bedtime he had let himself be tempted by laziness. And now his punishment is at hand.

He sits up in bed and tries to think. The door is locked. There are bars on the window. Impossible to get out. He crawls to the floor and makes rowing motions with his hands under the bed, looking for the pot that he knows isn't there.

He lies down and gets up again. Better to move around, to walk, to stamp than to sleep. With his two fists he compresses his expanding belly.

"Mama, Mama!" he says feebly, afraid she might hear him, because if Madame Lepic should appear, Poil de Carotte would be cured on the spot and seem to be joking at her expense. All he wants is to be able to say next day, without lying, that he called.

And even if he wanted to, how could he cry out? His efforts to ward off disaster use up all his strength.

Soon an extreme pang starts Poil de Carotte dancing. He bumps into the wall and bounces back. He collides with the iron bedstead. He bumps into the chair, he bumps into the fireplace. Abruptly he pulls up the apron and throws himself down between the andirons, convulsed, defeated, utterly happy. The blackness is thicker than ever.

III

Poil de Carotte has fallen asleep only at dawn and is still lying in bed when Madame Lepic opens the door. She screws up her nose.

"What an odd smell!" she says.

"Good morning, Mama," says Poil de Carotte.

Madame Lepic rips off the sheets, sniffs in every corner, and soon finds what she was looking for.

"I was sick and there wasn't any pot," Poil de Carotte hastens to explain. This strikes him as his best line of defense.

"Liar!" says Madame Lepic.

She leaves the room and comes back with a chamber pot which she hides from his view and slips deftly under the bed. Then she pulls Poil de Carotte out of the bed, calls the family in, and cries out:

"What have I done to be punished with such a child?"

She brings in rags and a pail of water. She floods the fireplace as though putting out the fire, she shakes the bedclothes and cries out plaintively for air, air. And in between she shakes her fist in Poil de Carotte's face.

"You little wretch! You're out of your mind. You're degenerate! You've turned into an animal. But if you gave an animal a chamber pot, it would know how to use it. All you can think of is flopping down in fireplaces. God is my witness, you're driving me insane, I shall die insane."

Barefoot in his nightgown, Poil de Carotte looks at the pot. Last night there wasn't any and now there is, right here at the foot of the bed. The empty white pot dazzles him, to persist in not seeing it would take more nerve than he's got.

The family is in despair, facetious neighbors troop in, the postman arrives. All tease him and beset him with questions.

"Word of honor!" Poil de Carotte finally answers with his eyes on the chamber pot. "I just don't know. Have it your own way."

THE RABBITS

T HERE'S NO melon left for you," says Madame Lepic. "Anyway, you're like me, you don't care for melon."

"Isn't that lucky!" says Poil de Carotte to himself.

His likes and dislikes are imposed on him. In general he is supposed to like only what his mother likes. When the cheese is served:

"I'm sure Poil de Carotte won't have any," says Madame Lepic.

"If she's sure," says Poil de Carotte to himself, "there's no use trying." Moreover, he knows it would be dangerous.

And besides, hasn't he plenty of opportunity to satisfy his wildest fancies in places known to him alone? Over the dessert, Madame Lepic says to him, "Go take these melon rinds to your rabbits."

Poil de Carotte goes out very slowly, holding the plate carefully level for fear of dropping any of the rinds. As he enters the rabbit house, the rabbits with their bully-boy hair-dos, with one ear down over the other and and their noses in the air, crowd around him, sitting up on their hind ends and holding their forepaws out stiff as if they were about to play the drum.

"Just a moment, please," says Poil de Carotte. "Share and share alike."

Sitting down on a pile of droppings, of groundsel gnawed to the root, of cabbage stalks and mallow leaves, he gives them the melon seeds and drinks the juice himself: it's as sweet as sweet wine.

Then with his teeth he scrapes off all the sweet yellow that his family has left on the slices, the part that melts in the mouth, and passes the green to the rabbits sitting in a circle.

He closes the door of the little hut.

The after-dinner sun threads through the holes in the tiles and dips the ends of its beams into the cool shade.

THE MATTOCK

BIG BROTHER Felix and Poil de Carotte are working side by side. Each has his mattock. Big brother Felix's was made to order by the blacksmith, out of iron. Poil de Carotte made his all by himself, out of wood. They are hard at work in the garden, vying with one another in enthusiasm. Suddenly, just when he least expects it (accidents always happen at that precise moment), a mattock strikes Poil de Carotte square in the forehead.

A few moments later big brother Felix has to be carried into the house and laid down gingerly on the bed. He has fainted at the sight of his little brother's blood. The whole family is there on tiptoes, sighing anxiously.

"Where are the salts?"

"A little fresh water, please, to moisten his temples."

Poil de Carotte climbs up on a chair to look over their

shoulders, between their heads. His forehead is bandaged in a cloth that is already red, oozing and dripping blood.

Monsieur Lepic on catching sight of him: "That's quite a crack you got."

And sister Ernestine who dressed his wound: "It went in like butter."

He didn't yell because he'd been told that it doesn't help.

But now big brother Felix opens one eye, then the other. He's had a bad fright, nothing more. As gradually the color comes back into his cheeks, the anguish of the others is dispelled.

"You'll never change," says Madame Lepic to Poil de Carotte. "Couldn't you watch out, you little fool?"

THE CARBINE

MONSIEUR LEPIC says to his sons:
"One carbine is enough for the two of you. Brothers who love each other share everything."

"Yes, Papa," big brother Felix replies, "we'll share the carbine. Actually I'll be satisfied if Poil de Carotte lends it to me now and then."

Poil de Carotte doesn't say Yes and he doesn't say No. He has his suspicions.

Monsieur Lepic takes the carbine out of its green case and asks, "Which one of you will carry it first? I'd think it ought to be the older."

BIG BROTHER FELIX

Poil de Carotte can have the honor. Let him take it first.

MONSIEUR LEPIC

Felix, you're behaving very nicely this morning. I'll remember this.

Monsieur Lepic lodges the carbine on Poil de Carotte's shoulder.

MONSIEUR LEPIC

All right, boys. Get going. Have a good time and don't fight.

POIL DE CAROTTE

Should we take the dog?

MONSIEUR LEPIC

No point in it. You can take turns at being the dog. Besides, hunters like you don't wound their game: they kill it outright.

Poil de Carotte and big brother Felix start out. Their outfit is simple, their everyday clothes. They are sorry not to have boots, but Monsieur Lepic often tells them that real hunters won't have anything to do with boots. Your true hunter's pants hang down over his heels. He never rolls them up. He tramps through muck and over plowed fields, and soon boots develop. They reach all the way up to the knees—solid, natural boots which the maid has orders to leave untouched.

"I bet you won't come home empty-handed," says big brother Felix.

"I hope not," says Poil de Carotte.

He feels an itch in the hollow of his shoulder and can't make himself lay his gun stock against it.

"Hey," says big brother Felix, "I'll let you carry it as long as you please."

"You're a good brother," says Poil de Carotte.

When a flock of sparrows darts up, he motions his big brother Felix not to move. The sparrows flit from hedge to hedge. Hunched forward, the two hunters approach soundlessly as though the sparrows were asleep. The birds refuse to stay put. Twittering, they fly off to another perch. The two hunters straighten up; big brother Felix gives them a piece of his mind. Though his heart is pounding, Poil de Carotte seems less impatient. He dreads the moment when he will have to prove his skill.

What if he missed! Every delay comes as a relief.

But this time the sparrows seem to be waiting for him.

BIG BROTHER FELIX

Don't shoot. They're too far away.

POIL DE CAROTTE

Think so?

BIG BROTHER FELIX

Of course. Bending down gives you the wrong idea. You think you're on top of them. They're still a mile away.

And big brother Felix straightens up to prove that he's right. The sparrows take fright and fly away.

But one of them stays back, on the end of a swaying limb. He flicks his tail, jogs his head, and presents his belly.

POIL DE CAROTTE

I can get that one. Honestly, I'm positive.

BIG BROTHER FELIX

Get out of the way so I can see. Yes, you've really got a good shot there. Quick, lend me your carbine.

And already Poil de Carotte is standing there empty-handed, gaping, disarmed: in his place, in front of him, big brother Felix shoulders the carbine, aims, and fires. The sparrow falls.

It's like a magician's trick. A second ago Poil de Carotte was pressing the carbine to his heart. Suddenly he has lost it, and now he has it again, for big brother Felix has given it back. He's the dog now. He runs to retrieve the sparrow and says: "You're too slow. You've got to move a little faster."

POIL DE CAROTTE

Looks like it.

BIG BROTHER FELIX

What are you sulking about?

POIL DE CAROTTE

What do you expect me to do, sing?

BIG BROTHER FELIX

I don't see anything to complain about. We've got our sparrow, haven't we? Why, we might have missed it.

POIL DE CAROTTE

But I ...

BIG BROTHER FELIX

You or me, what difference does it make? I got one today, you'll get one tomorrow.

POIL DE CAROTTE

Oh, tomorrow.

BIG BROTHER FELIX

I promise.

POIL DE CAROTTE

I know. You always promise yesterday.

BIG BROTHER FELIX

I swear it. Now are you satisfied?

POIL DE CAROTTE

Oh well! . . . But why not try to find another sparrow right away; then I could try the carbine.

BIG BROTHER FELIX

No, it's too late. Let's get home so Mama can cook this one. I'll give it to you. Here, you big baby. Put it in your pocket and leave the beak sticking out.

The two hunters start for home. From time to time they meet a peasant who greets them with the remark: "Well, boys, I hope you haven't killed your father, at least."

Flattered, Poil de Carotte forgets his bitterness. They arrive, reconciled and triumphant. The moment he sees them, Monsieur Lepic cries out in astonishment, "Why, Poil de Carotte, you're still carrying the carbine. Have you been carrying it the whole time?"

"Almost," says Poil de Carotte.

THE MOLE

ALONG THE PATH Poil de Carotte finds a mole, as black as a chimney sweep. After playing with it a while, he decides to kill it. He throws it into the air a few times, deftly, so as to make it fall on a stone.

At first everything goes swimmingly.

Soon the mole's legs are broken, its head is split, its back is broken; it doesn't seem like a hard animal to kill.

Then, to Poil de Carotte's stupefaction, the mole stops dying. He throws it as high as a house, as high as the sky; it doesn't help.

"Blue blazes!" he says to himself. "He's not dead."

And actually the mole is writhing on the bloodstained stone; its fat belly is trembling like jelly, and the trembling gives an illusion of life.

"Blue blazes!" cries Poil de Carotte. "It's not dead yet." But he won't give up.

He picks it up, reviles it, and changes his method.

Red in the face, his eyes full of tears, he spits on the mole and dashes it against the stone with all his might.

But the shapeless belly is still moving.

And the more furiously Poil de Carotte hurls it, the less the mole seems to die.

LA LUZERNE

THE ALFALFA FIELD

POIL DE CAROTTE and big brother Felix are on their way home from Vespers. They are in a hurry because it's time for the four o'clock snack.

His big brother Felix will have a slice of bread with butter or jam on it, Poil de Carotte will have a slice of bread with nothing on it, because in his hurry to be a man he has declared in the presence of witnesses that he's not a fancy eater. He likes plain food; ordinarily he eats his dry bread with ostentation, and this very afternoon he is walking faster than brother Felix in the hope of being served first.

Sometimes the dry bread seems hard. Then Poil de Carotte flings himself on it as though attacking an enemy, seizes hold of it, bites into it, tears it with fierce jerks of his head, and sends the pieces flying. The family look on with curiosity.

He has the stomach of an ostrich, quite capable of

digesting stones or an old coin coated with verdigris. All in all he is not a difficult child to feed.

He presses the door handle. The door is locked.

"I don't think our parents are home," he says. "Give it a bang with your foot."

Cursing and swearing, big brother Felix attacks the heavy nail-studded door, which resounds at length. Then the two of them, combining their efforts, bruise their shoulders in vain.

POIL DE CAROTTE

They're definitely not home.

BIG BROTHER FELIX

But where are they?

POIL DE CAROTTE

We can't know everything. Let's sit down.

Seated on the cold steps, they feel uncommonly hungry. They express the violence of their hunger by yawning and beating their chests with their fists.

BIG BROTHER FELIX

If they think I'm going to wait for them!

POIL DE CAROTTE

I don't see what else we can do.

BIG BROTHER FELIX

I won't wait for them. Think I want to die of starvation? I want to eat right away, anything, grass for instance.

POIL DE CAROTTE

Grass! That's an idea. And it will serve our parents right.

BIG BROTHER FELIX

Why not? People eat salad, don't they? Between you and me, alfalfa, for instance, is just as tender as salad. It's salad without oil and vinegar.

POIL DE CAROTTE

And you don't have to mix it.

BIG BROTHER FELIX

You want to bet that I'll eat some alfalfa and you won't?

POIL DE CAROTTE

Why you and not me?

BIG BROTHER FELIX

No kidding, you want to bet?

POIL DE CAROTTE

But why don't we ask the neighbors for a slice of bread with sour milk on it?

BIG BROTHER FELIX

I'd rather have alfalfa.

POIL DE CAROTTE

Let's go.

Soon they are looking upon the appetizing greenness of the alfalfa field. They step in, and a moment later they are joyfully dragging their feet, crushing the soft stalks and marking narrow paths that will leave people puzzled and wondering, "What kind of an animal has been through here?"

The coolness pierces their breeches and soon they feel a numbness in their calves.

They stop in the middle of the field and throw themselves down on their stomachs.

"It feels good," says big brother Felix.

The grass tickles their faces, and they laugh as they used to do when they slept in the same bed and Monsieur Lepic called in from the next room: "Will you miserable brats kindly go to sleep?"

They forget their hunger and begin to swim, sidestroke, dog paddle, breaststroke. Only their heads emerge. With their hands and feet they cut through the little green waves which offer slight resistance. But this is dead water that doesn't close in behind them.

"I'm up to my chin," says big brother Felix.

"Look how fast I go," says Poil de Carotte.

They have to rest, to relish their happiness more calmly.

Propped up on their elbows, they follow the raised tunnels of the moles, zigzagging barely under the ground as veins do under the skins of old people. For a time they disappear from sight, then the passageways open out into a clearing where the devil's-guts, a malignant parasite, the plague of the alfalfa fields, unfolds its beard of red tendrils. Here the molehills form a tiny village of wigwamlike huts.

"This is all very well," says big brother Felix, "but what about eating? I'm starting in. Watch you don't take any of mine."

He describes an arc with his arm for radius.

"I've got plenty out here," says Poil de Carotte.

The two heads vanish. Nobody would ever guess they were there.

The wind breathes sweetly, turning over the thin alfalfa leaves, disclosing the pale underside, and the whole field is traversed by shudders.

Big brother Felix tears up whole armfuls of fodder, buries his head in it, and pretends to gorge himself, making a sound like the jaws of an inexperienced calf stowing it away. He pretends to devour everything, roots and all, for he knows that life is hard. And Poil de Carotte takes him seriously, but, daintier in his tastes, chooses only the best leaves.

He bends them with the tip of his nose, guides them to his mouth, and chews them with deliberation.

Why hurry?

Nobody's waiting for their table. There's no fire.

And grinding his teeth, his tongue steeped in bitterness, his stomach rising to his throat, he swallows, he makes a feast of it.

THE DRINKING CUP

POIL DE CAROTTE will never drink again at table. In only a few days' time he has overcome the habit of drinking with an ease that amazes his family and friends It begins one morning when Madame Lepic is pouring him wine as usual. "No, thank you, Mama," he says. "I'm not thirsty."

At the evening meal he repeats, "No, thank you, Mama, I'm not thirsty."

"You're getting thrifty," says Madame Lepic. "That will leave all the more for the rest of us."

All this first day he goes without drinking because the air is mild and he simply isn't thirsty.

Next day as Madame Lepic is setting the table, she asks him:

"Are you going to drink today, Poil de Carotte?"

"I really don't know."

"As you wish," says Madame Lepic. "If you want your cup, you can get it out of the cupboard."

Whether from caprice, absentmindedness, or fear of serving himself, he doesn't get it.

The others are beginning to be astonished.

"You're improving yourself," says Madame Lepic. "That gives you one more talent."

"A rare and precious one," says Monsieur Lepic. "It will come in handy later on, someday when you're alone, lost in the desert without a camel."

Big brother Felix and sister Ernestine lay bets.

SISTER ERNESTINE

I bet he goes a whole week without drinking.

BIG BROTHER FELIX

Go on, he'll be doing all right if he holds out for three days, until Sunday.

"No," says Poil de Carotte with a knowing smile. "I'll never drink again. I won't have to because I'm never thirsty. Look at the rabbits and guinea pigs. Are they so remarkable?"

"You're no guinea pig," says big brother Felix.

Offended, Poil de Carotte decides to show his mettle. Madame Lepic keeps forgetting his cup. He wouldn't dream of asking for it. With equal indifference he accepts their ironic compliments and their expressions of sincere admiration.

"He's sick or he's crazy," is one opinion.

Another: "He's drinking in secret."

But the novelty wears off. Little by little Poil de Carotte stops sticking out his tongue to prove that it's not dry.

The family and neighbors lose interest. Only a few strangers still raise their hands to high heaven when they hear about it. "No, you exaggerate. You can't go against nature."

The doctor is consulted. He declares that the case does seem odd but that, come to think of it, nothing is impossible.

And Poil de Carotte, who had feared he was going to suffer, discovers to his surprise that with obstinate regularity one can do just about anything. He had thought he was exposing himself to a painful privation, attempting something incredibly difficult, and now he is not aware of any discomfort. He feels better than ever. What a pity that hunger cannot be defeated like thirst. He would feast, he would live on air.

He forgets all about his drinking cup. For a long while it stands unused. Then Honorine gets the idea of filling it with red tripoli to clean the candlesticks with.

LA MIE DE PAIN

THE PIECE OF BREAD

W HEN MONSIEUR LEPIC is in a good humor, he is not above entertaining his children. He tells them stories on the garden paths, and sometimes has big brother Felix and Poil de Carotte rolling on the ground with laughter. This morning they have reached the bursting point. But sister Ernestine comes out to announce that lunch is served, and that quiets them. Once the family is united, all faces cloud over.

As usual, they eat quickly, without taking time to breathe, as though someone were waiting for the table. Their meal is drawing to an end when Madame Lepic says, "Would you kindly pass me a piece of bread to finish my stewed fruit with?"

To whom is she speaking?

Ordinarily Madame Lepic helps herself and speaks only to the dog. She tells him about the price of vegetables and how hard it is nowadays to feed six people and an animal on very little money. "No," she says to Pyramus, who grunts affectionately and beats a tattoo on the doormat with his tail, "you can't imagine the time I have running this household. Just like a man. You think everything falls into the cook's lap. It's no worry of yours that butter has gone up and that eggs are out of sight."

But today Madame Lepic does something new. She addresses Monsieur Lepic directly. Unquestionably she has asked him for a piece of bread to finish her stewed fruit with. There's no room for doubt. In the first place, she is looking at him. In the second place, Monsieur Lepic has the bread beside him. In his astonishment he hesitates; then, with the tips of his fingers he picks up a smidgen of bread from his plate and solemnly, morosely, tosses it to Madame Lepic.

Farce or tragedy? Who knows?

Sister Ernestine feels humiliated for her mother and vaguely frightened.

"Papa's in good form today," says big brother Felix to himself, galloping merrily on the struts of his chair.

Hermetic, with bubbles on his lips, his ears full of sounds, and his cheeks puffed up with stewed apples, Poil de Carotte controls himself, but he is sure to explode if Madame Lepic doesn't leave the table instantly, for in the presence of her sons and daughter she has been treated like the lowest of the low.

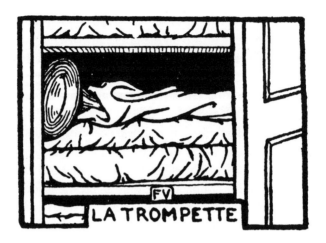

THE TRUMPET

THIS MORNING Monsieur Lepic has just got back from
Paris. He opens his trunk. Presents emerge for big brother
Felix and sister Ernestine, fine presents, precisely the ones
(how strange!) that they've been dreaming about all night.
Then, with his hands behind his back, Monsieur Lepic gives
Poil de Carotte a sly look and says, "And what about you?
What would you like better, a trumpet or a pistol?"

Poil de Carotte isn't a very daring child; actually he is
rather cautious. He would prefer a trumpet because it doesn't
explode in your hands. But he has always heard that a boy of
his size can only play seriously with guns, sabers, war
machines. At his age a boy is supposed to smell powder and
exterminate things. His father knows children: he has brought
the right thing.

"I'd sooner have a pistol," he says boldly, sure of guessing
right.

He even takes a chance and adds, "No use hiding it, I can see it."

"Ah!" says Monsieur Lepic with embarrassment. "You'd rather have a pistol? Then you've changed?"

Instantly Poil de Carotte corrects himself. "Oh no, Papa, I was only fooling. Set your mind at rest; I hate pistols. Give me my trumpet quick, I'll show you how I love to blow it."

MADAME LEPIC

Then why did you lie? To make your father feel badly, is that it? When you like trumpets, you don't say you like pistols, and especially you don't say that you see pistols when you don't see anything. You will have neither a pistol nor a trumpet, that will teach you a lesson. Take a good look at it: it has three red pompoms and a gold-fringed flag. That will do, you've seen enough. Now go in the kitchen and see if I'm there; run along, skedaddle, and whistle with your fingers.

High up in the closet, on a pile of white linen, rolled in its three red pompoms and gold-fringed flag, Poil de Carotte's trumpet waits for someone to blow it, as inaccessible, invisible, and silent as the trumpet of the Last Judgment.

LA MÈCHE

THE COWLICK

ON SUNDAY Madame Lepic insists on her sons going to Mass. That means dressing them up, and sister Ernestine in person presides over the operation, at the risk of being late herself. She chooses their ties, files their nails, and gives them their prayer books, always reserving the thicker one for Poil de Carotte. But most of all she pomades the brothers' hair.

It's a passion with her.

Poil de Carotte puts up with it like a sissy, but big brother Felix warns his sister that he's going to lose his temper one of these days. Consequently she cheats. "Oh," she says, "I forgot this time. I didn't do it on purpose. I swear that beginning next Sunday I won't put any on."

And each time she manages to inflict a fingerful.

"There's going to be trouble," says big brother Felix.

This morning, he sits there head down, wrapped in his towel. Sister Ernestine tricks him again and he doesn't notice.

"There," she says. "You've had your way, so don't grumble. See the closed jar on the mantelpiece. Aren't I nice? Anyway, it's only natural. With Poil de Carotte I ought to have cement, but you don't need any pomade. Your hair curls and waves all by itself. You've got a head like a cauliflower, and your part will last all day."

"Thank you," says big brother Felix.

He gets up unsuspecting. He neglects to check as usual by passing his hand over his hair.

Sister Ernestine puts on the rest of his clothes, administers a few finishing touches, and forces his hands into his white floss-silk gloves.

"You through?" says big brother Felix.

"You're as shiny as a prince," says sister Ernestine. "Nothing's missing but your cap. Go get it in the closet."

But big brother Felix loses his way. He passes the closet, runs to the sideboard, opens it, seizes a carafe full of water, and empties it calmly on his head.

"I warned you," he says. "I don't like to be made a fool of. You're too young to fool an old hand like me. If you ever try that again, I'll drown your pomade in the river."

His hair flattened, his Sunday suit dripping, he waits for them to change his clothes or for the sun to dry him, he doesn't care which.

"What a man!" says Poil de Carotte to himself, stunned with admiration. "He's not afraid of anybody. If I tried to imitate him, they'd only laugh. Better let them think I don't mind the pomade."

But though from long habit Poil de Carotte resigns himself, his hair, without consulting him, takes its revenge.

Forcibly flattened by the pomade, it plays dead for a time; then it comes to life and with an invisible thrust dents, cracks, and bursts its thin, glistening mold.

The effect is of thawing thatch.

And soon the first cowlick rises into the air, erect and free.

THE RIVER

I T'S ALMOST four o'clock. In frantic haste Poil de Carotte wakes up Monsieur Lepic and big brother Felix who are sleeping under the hazelnut bushes in the garden.

"Shouldn't we get started?" he asks.

BIG BROTHER FELIX

Let's go. You take the trunks.

MONSIEUR LEPIC

Isn't it still too hot?

BIG BROTHER FELIX

I like it when there's sun.

POIL DE CAROTTE

You'll be more comfortable by the water than here, Papa.
You can lie in the grass.

MONSIEUR LEPIC

You go ahead, but not too fast in this heat.

Poil de Carotte finds it hard to hold himself in; he has pins
and needles in his feet. Over his shoulder he is carrying his
own grimly plain trunks and big brother Felix's red and blue
trunks. Beaming from ear to ear, he talks and sings to himself
and jumps up at the branches. He swims in the air and says to
big brother Felix:
"Think the water will be all right? Boy, will we splash and
kick!"
"Let's not gloat too soon," says big brother Felix, scornful
and knowing what to expect.
And indeed Poil de Carotte's eagerness suddenly dies. Still
in the lead, he has just climbed a little stone wall. And all at
once the river is there in plain view. The time for laughing has
passed.
Cold lights play over the enchanted water. The lapping of
the ripples sounds like chattering teeth, and there is a brack-
ish smell in the air.
Now he will have to go in, stay in, and pass the time while
Monsieur Lepic counts the regulation number of minutes on
his watch. Poil de Carotte shivers. He has been lashing his
courage to keep it up, but once again it fails him when he
needs it. The sight of the water, so alluring in the distance,
makes his heart sink.
Poil de Carotte goes off to one side to undress. The idea is
not so much to hide his skinniness and his feet, as to do his
trembling alone and unabashed.

He takes off one garment at a time, folds it and lays it carefully on the grass. He knots his shoelaces and takes forever to undo them. He puts on his trunks and removes his short shirt. But since he is sweating like a stick of apple sugar under its wrapper, he waits a little while longer.

Big brother Felix has already taken possession of the river and is punishing it masterfully, giving it great clouts and kicks, making it foam and, standing formidable in midstream, chasing the flocks of angry waves toward the shore.

"Given up?" asks Monsieur Lepic.

"I was drying off," says Poil de Carotte.

Finally he makes up his mind. He sits down on the bank and feels the water with a big toe crushed by tight shoes. At the same time he rubs his stomach, which may not have finished digesting. Then he slides down over the roots.

They scratch his calves, his thighs, his buttocks. When the water is up to his waist, he thinks he'll climb back out again. He feels as if a wet string had rolled around his body as around a top. But the hummock he is standing on gives way and Poil de Carotte falls and disappears. He flails about and picks himself up, coughing, spitting, choking, blinded and stunned.

"You're quite a diver, my boy," says Monsieur Lepic.

"I guess so," says Poil de Carotte, "though I don't like it much. The water stays in my ears; I'm going to have a headache."

He looks for a place where he can learn to swim, that is, move his arms while his knees crawl on the sand.

"You're in too much of a hurry," says Monsieur Lepic. "Don't thrash your fists as if you were tearing your hair out. Move your legs, they're not doing anything."

"It's harder to swim without using the legs," says Poil de Carotte.

But big brother Felix keeps molesting him; he won't let him concentrate.

"Come over here, Poil de Carotte. There are deep places. It's over my head, I'm sinking. Look. Now you see me. Look sharp. Now you don't. Now go over toward the willow. Don't move. I bet I'll reach you in ten strokes."

"I'm counting," says Poil de Carotte shivering, his shoulders out of water, as motionless as a real finishing post.

He bends down again to swim. But big brother Felix climbs on his back, dives off, and says: "Now climb on my back if you want to."

"Let me take my lesson in peace," says Poil de Carotte.

"All right, boys," Monsieur Lepic cries. "Out with you. Come and have a drop of rum."

"So soon?" says Poil de Carotte.

He no longer wants to come out. He hasn't taken full advantage of his bath. Now that he has to leave the water, it doesn't frighten him any more. The lead in his heart has suddenly turned to feathers. He thrashes about with frantic courage, defying danger, ready to risk his life to save someone. He even ducks under on purpose in order to savor the terror of a drowning man.

"Hurry," cries Monsieur Lepic, "or big brother Felix will drink up all the rum."

Although Poil de Carotte doesn't like rum, he says, "Nobody can have my share."

And he drinks it like an old soldier.

MONSIEUR LEPIC

You haven't washed properly. There's still smut on your ankles.

POIL DE CAROTTE

It's only dirt, Papa.

MONSIEUR LEPIC

No, it's smut.

POIL DE CAROTTE

Do you want me to go back in, Papa?

MONSIEUR LEPIC

You'll get rid of it tomorrow. We'll be back.

POIL DE CAROTTE

What luck! If only the weather holds out!

He rubs himself vaguely with the bits of the towel that big brother Felix has left dry. His head swimming, his throat corroded, he goes into gales of laughter. His brother and Monsieur Lepic are saying such funny things about his pudgy toes.

HONORINE

MADAME LEPIC

How old are you, anyway, Honorine?

HONORINE

Sixty-seven come All Saints' Day, Madame Lepic.

MADAME LEPIC

My poor old dear, you're getting old.

HONORINE

It doesn't mean a thing as long as I'm able to work. Never been sick a day in my life. I'm as strong as a horse, stronger if you ask me.

MADAME LEPIC

Let me tell you something, Honorine. You'll die suddenly.

One afternoon on your way back from the river, your basket will feel heavier, your wheelbarrow will be harder to push than other days. You'll fall on your knees between the shafts, with your nose in the wet washing, and that will be the end. When they pick you up, you'll be dead.

HONORINE

You make me laugh, Madame Lepic; don't you worry, there's life in the old girl yet.

MADAME LEPIC

You're a little stooped, but that's nothing; the washing is less tiring when you haven't so far to bend. But it's a pity your sight is failing. Don't say it isn't, Honorine. I've noticed it for some time now.

HONORINE

How can you say such things? My eyes are as keen as they were on my wedding day.

MADAME LEPIC

All right. Open the cupboard and give me a plate, any plate. If you dry your dishes properly, how do you account for that mist?

HONORINE

It's damp in the cupboard.

MADAME LEPIC

And I suppose there are fingers in the cupboard that crawl around on the dishes? Look at that mark.

HONORINE

What mark, Madame? I don't see a thing.

MADAME LEPIC

That's just what I've been saying, Honorine. Listen to me.
I don't say that you're getting slack, that would be unjust; I
don't know of a harder-working woman for miles around.
Only you're getting old. I'm getting old, too: we're all getting
old, and the time comes when good intentions aren't enough.
I'm willing to bet that you sometimes feel a kind of film over
your eyes. And rub as you may, you can't get rid of it.

HONORINE

All the same, I keep them wide-open, and it's not as if I had
my head in a pail of water.

MADAME LEPIC

Yes, it is, Honorine, take it from me. Only yesterday you
gave Monsieur Lepic a dirty glass. I didn't say anything for
fear of hurting your feelings and making a scene. Monsieur
Lepic didn't say anything either. He never says anything, but
nothing escapes him. You may think he doesn't care; you're
mistaken. He takes note, and everything he sees is graven on
his mind. He just pushed away your glass with his finger, he
controlled himself and went through lunch without drinking.
I suffered for you and for him.

HONORINE

Blessed if I can see why Monsieur Lepic should use kid
gloves with his maid. He only had to speak up, I'd have
changed his glass.

MADAME LEPIC

That may be, Honorine, but smarter people than you haven't
been able to make Monsieur Lepic say anything when he's
made up his mind not to. I myself have given up trying. But
that's not the question. I repeat: every day your sight is

getting a little dimmer. There's not too much harm in it when it comes to the heavy work, the washing for instance, but you're not up to delicate work anymore. Regardless of the extra expense, I'd gladly look around for someone to help you . . .

HONORINE

I could never stand another woman underfoot, Madame Lepic.

MADAME LEPIC

You've taken the words out of my mouth. Well then? Frankly, what do you advise?

HONORINE

We'll worry along all right until I pass away.

MADAME LEPIC

Pass away? What are you thinking of, Honorine? You'll bury us all, and I hope you do. Do you suppose I'm reckoning with your death?

HONORINE

I hope you're not thinking of sending me away for a little smudge on a glass. In the first place, I won't leave your house unless you throw me out. And then what? Do you want me to die like a dog?

MADAME LEPIC

Who's said anything about sending you away, Honorine? Why, you're all red in the face. Here we've just been having a friendly chat, and you get angry and say the silliest things ever.

HONORINE

Gracious, what am I to think?

MADAME LEPIC

And I? It's not your fault if your sight is failing, or mine. I hope the doctor will cure you. It's been known to happen. Meanwhile, who is worse off, you or I? You don't even realize that your sight is failing. And the housekeeping suffers. I'm only telling you out of charity, to prevent accidents, and also because I have the right, it seems to me, to make a gentle remark now and then.

HONORINE

Of course you have. Go right ahead, Madame Lepic. For a minute I thought I was out in the street. You've set my mind at rest. I'll be careful about the dishes, you can count on that.

MADAME LEPIC

Have I ever asked for anything else? I'm not as bad as they make me out to be, Honorine, and I won't dispense with your services unless you absolutely oblige me to.

HONORINE

When that happens, Madame Lepic, you won't have to say a word. Right now I feel I can make myself useful; I'd call it an injustice if you sent me away. But the day I see I'm a burden to you and I'm not even able to heat a kettle of water on the stove, I'll leave of my own free will; nobody will have to tell me.

MADAME LEPIC

But never forget, Honorine, that there'll always be a dish of soup for you here.

HONORINE

No, Madame Lepic, no soup; only bread. Ever since mother Maïtte took to eating nothing but bread, she's given up dying.

MADAME LEPIC

And did you know that she's at least a hundred? And let me tell you another thing, Honorine. Beggars are better off than we are, take it from me.

HONORINE

If you say so, Madame Lepic, I say so too.

LA MARMITE

THE KETTLE

P OIL DE CAROTTE doesn't often get a chance to make himself useful to the family. Tucked away in a corner, he waits for one to turn up. He is capable of listening without preconceived opinion. Then, at the right moment, he emerges from the shadow, cool and levelheaded, keeping his wits about him when everyone else is befuddled by emotion, and takes matters in hand.

He senses that Madame Lepic needs an intelligent, reliable helper, though of course she is too proud to admit it. Their cooperation will be tacit, and Poil de Carotte will have to act without encouragement or hope of reward.

That is the course he resolves to take.

From morning to night a kettle hangs from the pothook in the fireplace. In the winter, when a great deal of hot water is needed, it bubbles on a blazing fire and is often emptied and filled.

In the summer, hot water is used only for washing the dishes after meals. The rest of the time, the kettle simmers to no purpose with a soft continuous purr, while under its scarred belly smoke rises from two scarcely smoldering logs.

Sometimes Honorine fails to hear the purring. She leans over and listens.

"It's all steamed away," she says.

She pours a bucketful of water into the kettle, moves the two logs closer together, and stirs the coals. Soon the soft music starts up again and Honorine, her mind at rest, busies herself somewhere else.

If you were to say:

"Honorine, why do you heat water you have no use for? Take away the kettle. Let the fire go out. You burn wood as if it cost nothing. Think of all the poor people who freeze when the cold weather sets in. You who've always been so thrifty—"

She would shake her head. She has always seen a kettle hanging on the end of the pothook. She has always heard the water boiling and when the kettle is empty, rain or shine, she has always filled it up again.

And now she has no need to touch the kettle or even to see it; she knows it by heart. She only has to listen, and if the kettle is silent, she throws in a bucketful of water as though stringing a bead; she's done it so often she never misses.

Today for the first time she misses.

All the water falls in the fire and, like some animal furious at being awakened, hot ashes leap up at Honorine, enveloping, choking, and burning her.

She screams and backs away, sneezing and spitting.

"Holy Mary!" she says. "It's like the Devil come up from underground."

Her eyes glued shut and burning, she gropes her way with blackened hands into the night of the fireplace.

"Ah, now I see!" she cries in consternation. "The kettle isn't there."

"Indeed it isn't," she says. "I can't understand it. It was there a minute ago. It must have been, it was whistling like a fife."

Somebody must have taken it when she was turning her back to shake an apronful of peelings out the window.

But who could it have been?

"What's all the noise, Honorine?"

"Noise, noise!" cries Honorine. "Who wouldn't make noise, I've been practically boiled. Look at my sabots and my petticoat; look at my hands. There's mud on my jacket and coals in my pocket."

MADAME LEPIC

What interests me is that puddle dripping out of the fireplace. That's going to make a fine mess.

HONORINE

Why should they steal my kettle without telling me? Was it you by any chance?

MADAME LEPIC

That kettle belongs to all of us, Honorine. Are you going to stand there and tell me that I or Monsieur Lepic or my children are supposed to ask you for permission to use it.

HONORINE

I'm so angry I could say anything.

MADAME LEPIC

At us or yourself, my good Honorine? Or at whom else? I'm not curious, but I'd like to know. You exasperate me. On the pretext that the kettle has disappeared, you calmly throw a whole pail of water in the fire, and you're so stubborn that instead of admitting your clumsiness you put the blame on others, on me for instance. My word, that's going a little too far!

HONORINE

Poil de Carotte, child, do you know where my kettle is?

MADAME LEPIC

How would he know, a child without a thought in his head? Forget about your kettle. You'd do better to remember what you said yesterday: "The day I see that I can't even heat water, I'll leave of my own free will; no one will have to tell me." Of course I knew your eyes were bad, but I didn't think your condition was desperate. I have nothing to add, Honorine; put yourself in my place. You are as well aware of the situation as I am; draw your own conclusions. Oh, don't mind me, cry if you feel like it. I could do with a cry myself.

RETICENCE

"Mama! Honorine!"

What does Poil de Carotte want now? He's going to spoil it all. Fortunately his mother's cold stare stops him short.

What's the use of saying: "I did it, Honorine."?

Nothing can save the old woman. She's lost her eyesight, that's her hard luck. Sooner or later she'd have to give in. A confession from him would only make her feel worse. Let her leave and, instead of suspecting Poil de Carotte, imagine she has been struck by the inexorable hand of fate.

And why say to Madame Lepic: "Mama, I did it."?

Why pride himself on a good deed and beg to be honored with a smile? Besides, it would be risky, for he knows that Madame Lepic is perfectly capable of publicly disavowing him. Better mind his own business, or rather pretend to help his mother and Honorine look for the kettle.

And when for a moment all three join in looking for it, he

[69]

is the most energetic. Madame Lepic is first to lose interest and give up.

Honorine resigns herself and goes off mumbling, and soon Poil de Carotte, whom conscience has almost brought to disaster, goes back into himself as into a sheath, like an instrument of justice that is no longer needed.

AGATHE

AGATHE

AGATHE, a granddaughter of Honorine, takes her place.
Poil de Carotte observes the newcomer with curiosity.
For a few days she will distract the Lepics' attention from
himself.

"Agathe," says Madame Lepic, "knock before you come in,
which doesn't mean you should pound like a horse and bash
the door in."

"Here we go," says Poil de Carotte to himself. "But let's
wait until lunch time."

They eat in the big kitchen. A napkin over one arm, Agathe
is standing ready to run from stove to cupboard, from cupboard to table, for she is quite incapable of walking with dignity. She prefers to run; she puffs and pants and the blood
rushes to her head.

Moreover she talks too fast, laughs too loud, and is too
eager to do the right thing.

Monsieur Lepic sits down first, unknots his napkin, pushes his plate toward the platter which is in front of him, helps himself to meat and gravy, and moves back his plate. He pours himself wine and with bent back and lowered eyes eats moderately, with indifference, today as every other day.

When the platter is changed, he leans forward in his chair and wiggles his leg.

Madame Lepic serves herself and the children, first big brother Felix because he is ravenous, then sister Ernestine because she is the eldest, and finally Poil de Carotte who is at the end of the table.

Poil de Carotte never asks for seconds, as if there were an express rule against it. A single portion ought to be enough. If anything is offered him, he accepts; without ever drinking, he stuffs himself on rice which he doesn't like, in order to please Madame Lepic who alone of all the family is very fond of it.

Big brother Felix and sister Ernestine are more independent. If they desire a second helping, they push their plates toward the platter like Monsieur Lepic.

But no one talks.

"What's wrong with them?" says Agathe to herself.

There's nothing wrong with them. It's simply the way they are.

She stands there with her arms apart, in front of this one, in front of that one, unable to repress a yawn.

Monsieur Lepic eats slowly, as though chewing ground glass.

Madame Lepic, though more talkative than a magpie between meals, gives her orders at table with gestures and signs of the head.

Sister Ernestine raises her eyes to the ceiling.

Big brother Felix molds his bread pulp and Poil de Carotte, who no longer has a cup, thinks only of not emptying his plate too quickly, which is gluttony, or too slowly, which is daw-dling. The problem involves complex calculations.

Suddenly Monsieur Lepic gets up to fill the carafe with water.

"I'd have done that," says Agathe.

Or rather, she doesn't say it, she only thinks it. She is stricken with the general ailment. Her tongue is heavy, she doesn't dare open her mouth, but feeling at fault, she watches more attentively than ever.

Monsieur Lepic has hardly any bread left. This time Agathe won't let him get ahead of her. She watches him so intensely that she forgets the others and Madame Lepic calls her to order with a dry: "Agathe, are you growing a branch?"

"Here you are, Madame."

And she moves in all directions without taking her eyes off Monsieur Lepic. She is determined to win him over with her attentions, to prove herself.

The time has come.

As Monsieur Lepic bites into his last mouthful of bread, she gallops to the cupboard and brings back a five-pound crown, uncut. She holds it out to him joyfully, delighted at having anticipated the master's desires.

But Monsieur Lepic folds his napkin, leaves the table, puts on his hat, and goes out into the garden to smoke a cigarette.

Once he has finished eating, he doesn't start in again.

Transfixed, stupefied, clutching the five-pound crown to her stomach, Agathe looks like a wax dummy advertising a lifesaver factory.

THE PROGRAM

T**HAT FLOORS YOU**," says Poil de Carotte as soon Agathe and he are alone in the kitchen. "Don't be discouraged. You'll see plenty more. But where are you going with those bottles?"

"To the cellar, Monsieur Poil de Carotte."

POIL DE CAROTTE

Oh no, the cellar is my job. The steps are bad. A woman could slip and break her neck. I've been the cellar man ever since I've been able to get down them. I can tell a red seal from a blue seal.

I do a little business selling the old casks, rabbit skins too, and I give my mother the money.

We had better come to an understanding, so as not to interfere with each other's duties.

In the morning I let the dog out and give him his soup. At

night I whistle for him to come in and go to bed. If he's roaming the streets, I wait for him.

In addition, Mama promised that I would always get to close the henhouse.

I pull up plants for the animals; you've got to know them. I shake the earth off them with my foot, to plug up the holes with again.

For exercise I help my father sawing wood.

I finish off game birds when he brings them back alive; you will help Ernestine pluck them.

I open up the bellies of the fish, clean them, and squash their bladders with my heel.

But you'll scale them and draw pails of water from the well.

I help them to wind off thread from the hank.

I grind the coffee.

When Monsieur Lepic takes off his soiled boots, I carry them out to the corridor, but only sister Ernestine is entitled to bring him his slippers that she herself embroidered.

I run the long errands, like going to the druggist's or the doctor's.

You will only have to chase around the village attending to the day-to-day shopping.

But for two or three hours a day, rain or shine, you will have to wash clothes in the river. Poor thing, that will be the hardest part of your work. There's nothing I can do about it. All the same, when I'm free, I'll try to give you a hand now and then spreading out the washing on the hedge.

That reminds me: a piece of advice. Never lay your washing on the fruit trees. Monsieur Lepic won't say a word, he'll just flip it onto the ground, and Madame Lepic, to keep you busy, will make you wash it all over again.

Be careful about the shoes. Plenty of fat on the hunting boots and very little polish on the town shoes. It burns the leather.

Don't waste your time on muddy breeches. Monsieur Lepic claims that mud preserves them. He walks through plowed fields without turning up the bottoms. I prefer to turn mine up when Monsieur Lepic takes me with him and I carry the game bag.

"Poil de Carotte," he says. "You'll never be a real hunter."

And Madame Lepic says: "Watch out for your ears if you get dirty."

It's a matter of taste.

All in all you won't be too badly off. During my vacation we'll share the work and when my sister, my brother and I go back to school, there'll be less of it. It evens out.

You won't find any of us really mean. Ask our friends: they'll all swear to you that my sister Ernestine is an angel, that my brother Felix has a heart of gold; they'll tell you about Monsieur Lepic's fairness and sound judgment, and Madame Lepic's unusual talents as a cook. Maybe you'll find me the most difficult member of the family. But all in all I'm no worse than anybody else. You just have to know how to handle me. What's more, I try, I correct myself; without false modesty, I am improving, and with a little effort on your part we'll get along fine.

No, stop calling me monsieur, call me Poil de Carotte like everybody else. It's shorter than Monsieur Lepic Junior. Only kindly no terms of endearment like your grandmother Honorine, whom I detested because she rubbed me the wrong way.

THE BLIND MAN

WITH THE TIP of his cane he knocks discreetly at the door.

MADAME LEPIC

Now what does he want?

MONSIEUR LEPIC

As if you didn't know. He wants his ten sous; it's his day. Let him in.

Morosely Madame Lepic opens the door and pulls the blind man in by the arm, brusquely because of the cold.

"Greetings all here," says the blind man.

He moves toward the center of the room. His cane takes little steps over the flags as though chasing mice, and encounters a chair. The blind man sits down and holds out his frozen hands toward the stove.

Monsieur Lepic takes a fifty-centime piece and says, "Here you are."

Taking no further notice of the blind man, he goes on reading his paper.

Poil de Carotte is enjoying himself. Huddled in his corner, he is looking at the blind man's sabots: they are thawing, sending out rivulets in all directions.

Madame Lepic sees them.

"Lend me your sabots, old man," she says.

She takes them to the fireplace. Too late, they have left a puddle. The blind man is apprehensive. His feet, smelling of dampness, rise up, first one, then the other, and push away the muddy snow.

Poil de Carotte scratches the floor with his fingernail, beckons to the dirty water to run in his direction, points out the deep cracks.

"Now that he's got his money," says Madame Lepic without fear of being heard, "what is he waiting for?"

But the blind man is talking politics, first timidly, then with aplomb. When the words won't come, he shakes his cane and burns his fist on the stovepipe. He withdraws it quickly, the whites of his eyes rolling suspiciously behind a curtain of inexhaustible tears.

Now and then Monsieur Lepic, turning the pages of his paper, says, "Maybe so, Papa Tissier, maybe so, but can you be sure?"

"Can I be sure!" the blind man cries. "That's too much. Listen to me, Monsieur Lepic, and I'll tell you how I went blind."

"He'll never leave," says Madame Lepic.

And indeed the blind man is feeling better. He tells about his accident, stretches, and thaws from top to toe. The icicles in his veins dissolve and circulate. His clothes and limbs exude oil.

On the floor the puddle is growing; it's heading for Poil de Carotte, it's coming closer: he is its goal.

Soon he'll be able to play with it.

But Madame Lepic has devised a shrewd stratagem. She jostles the blind man in passing, pokes him with her elbow, steps on his feet, forces him back, maneuvers him into a spot between the sideboard and the closet, sheltered from the stove's radiation. Confused, the blind man gropes and gesticulates, his fingers climbing like animals. He sweeps the chimney of his darkness. New icicles form; he begins to freeze up again.

And the blind man finishes his story in a tearful voice.

"Yes, my friends, that was the end, no more eyes, no nothing, all black as an oven."

His cane gets away from him. That's what Madame Lepic has been waiting for. She hastens to pick it up and gives it back to the blind man—but she doesn't quite give it back.

He thinks he has it, but he hasn't.

By adroit feints she moves him again, puts on his sabots, and guides him toward the door.

She gives him a slight pinch to get partly even and pushes him out into the street, under the quilt of gray sky emptying out its snow, his face to the wind that is howling like a dog forgotten out of doors.

And before closing the door, Madame Lepic shouts at the blind man as if he were deaf, "Good-bye; don't forget your money; see you next Sunday if the weather is good and you're still of this world. My word, you're right, Papa Tissier, we never know who's going to live and who's going to die. We all have our troubles and the Lord help us all."

LE JOUR DE L'AN

NEW YEAR'S DAY

IT's snowing. You can't have a proper New Year's Day without snow.

Madame Lepic has prudently left the door to the yard barred. Already children are shaking at the latch, knocking on the door, first discreetly with their knuckles, then angrily with their sabots. Finally they give up hope and leave, walking backward, still looking up at the window from which Madame Lepic is peering out at them. The sound of their steps is blanketed in the snow.

Poil de Carotte jumps out of bed and runs out to wash without soap in the garden trough. It's frozen. He has to break the ice, and this first exercise suffuses his whole body with a heat healthier than the heat of a stove. He only pretends to wet his face. Since they say he's dirty even when he washes thoroughly, he only removes the thickest deposits.

Flushed and ready for the ceremony, he takes his place behind big brother Felix who is standing behind sister Ernestine, the eldest. The three of them enter the kitchen. Monsieur and Madame Lepic have just converged as though by chance.

Sister Ernestine kisses them and says:

"Good morning, Papa; good morning, Mama; I wish you a happy New Year, good health, and paradise at the end of your days."

Big brother Felix says the same, very fast, racing to the end of the sentence, and he too kisses them.

But Poil de Carotte takes a letter out of his cap. On the sealed envelope is written: "To my dear parents." No address. In one corner a bird of some rare species, rich in color, is darting through the air.

Poil de Carotte holds it out to Madame Lepic, who opens it. The paper is richly adorned with open blossoms and the border is so lacy that Poil de Carotte's pen has several times fallen into the holes, splashing the nearest word.

MONSIEUR LEPIC

But there's nothing for me.

POIL DE CAROTTE

It's for both of you; Mama will lend it to you.

MONSIEUR LEPIC

Then you love your mother more than me. If that's the case, search your pockets. Maybe you'll find a new ten-sou piece and maybe you won't.

POIL DE CAROTTE

Just a second, Mama's finished.

MADAME LEPIC

You have a style, but your handwriting's so bad I can't read it.

"Here, Papa," says Poil de Carotte eagerly, "it's your turn now."

While Poil de Carotte stands bolt upright waiting for the answer, Monsieur Lepic reads the letter once, twice, examines it at length as he always does, says "Ah! Ah!" and sets it down on the table.

It's no good for anything now. The effect is over. Now it belongs to everybody. Everybody can see and touch it. Sister Ernestine and big brother Felix take it by turns, looking for spelling mistakes. Poil de Carotte must have changed his pen at this point, it's more legible. Then they give it back to him.

He turns it over and over with an ungainly smile, as though asking: "Who wants it?"

Finally he puts it back in his cap.

The presents are given. Sister Ernestine gets a doll as big as herself or bigger, and big brother Felix a box of tin soldiers all ready to fight.

"I have a surprise for you," says Madame Lepic to Poil de Carotte.

POIL DE CAROTTE

Oh, what is it?

MADAME LEPIC

Why the silly question? If you know what it is, there's no point in my showing you.

POIL DE CAROTTE

May I never see God if I know what it is!

Solemn and self-assured, he raises his right hand. Madame Lepic opens the sideboard. Poil de Carotte pants with impatience. She plunges in her arm as far as the shoulder, then slowly, mysteriously, brings out a piece of yellow paper with a red candy pipe on it.

Without a moment's hesitation Poil de Carotte beams with joy. He knows the right thing to do. He will smoke in the presence of his parents, under the envious eyes (but after all, they can't have everything) of big brother Felix and sister Ernestine. Holding his red candy pipe between two fingers, he throws out his chest and cocks his head to one side. He rounds his lips, sucks in his cheeks, and takes a strong, long draw.

Then after releasing an enormous smoke cloud; "It's good," he says, "it draws fine."

ALLER ET RETOUR

ROUND TRIP

MESSIEURS LEPIC JR. and Mademoiselle Lepic are coming home on vacation. The moment he steps off the coach, Poil de Carotte sees his parents in the distance and begins to wonder: "Is it time to run to meet them?"

He hesitates: "It's too soon. I'd get out of breath. And besides, there's no point in overdoing it."

He keeps putting it off: "I'll start running there ... no, there ..."

He questions himself: "When should I take my cap off? Which one should I kiss first?"

But big brother Felix and sister Ernestine are there ahead of him, sharing the family caresses. By the time Poil de Carotte pulls up, there are hardly any left.

"What's this?" says Madame Lepic. "Still calling Monsieur Lepic 'Papa' at your age? Call him 'Father' and shake hands with him, it's more manly."

Then she kisses him once on the forehead so as to leave no room for jealousy.

Poil de Carotte is so glad to be on vacation he has tears in his eyes. It's often like that; he reacts the wrong way around.

When vacation is over (school is scheduled to open on the morning of Monday, October 2nd, with the Mass of the Holy Spirit) and Madame Lepic hears the diligence tinkling in the distance, she swoops down on her children and kisses them in one armful. But Poil de Carotte isn't in it. He waits patiently for his turn, his farewells ready-prepared, his hand already reaching for the straps of the box, so sad that he can't help singing a tune.

"Good-bye, Mother," he says with a dignified air.

"My goodness!" says Madame Lepic. "What's got into you? Would it be too much trouble to call me Mama like everybody else? Have you ever seen the likes of it? Still wet behind the ears and running at the nose, and he thinks he can put on airs."

Even so, she kisses him once on the forehead, so as to leave no room for jealousy.

LE PORTE-PLUME

THE PEN

St. Mark's Boarding Establishment, to which Monsieur Lepic has entrusted big brother Felix and Poil de Carotte, sends its boys to the nearby high school for their classes.

They cover the same itinerary four times a day. It's a pleasant walk in good weather and on rainy days so brief that it leaves the boys more refreshed than wet; in short, it's excellent for their health at all times.

This morning, as languidly dragging their feet they return from the high school, one of the boys says to Poil de Carotte, who has his eyes to the ground: "Poil de Carotte, look, your father."

Monsieur Lepic likes to surprise his children. He turns up without writing, and one fine day they see him on the corner across the street with his hands behind his back and a cigarette between his lips.

Poil de Carotte and big brother Felix leave the procession and run to join their father.

"My goodness!" says Poil de Carotte, "If there's anybody I wasn't thinking of!"

"You think of me when you see me," says Monsieur Lepic.

Poil de Carotte wants to make an affectionate reply. But he's so busy he can't think of anything. Standing up on tiptoes, he tries to kiss his father. At the first attempt he barely touches his father's beard with his lips. But automatically Monsieur Lepic raises his head as though to avoid him. Then he bends down, but retreats again, and Poil de Carotte who was aiming for his cheek misses it. He barely grazes his nose and kisses the void. He stops trying and, already dismayed, attempts to account for his father's strange reception.

"Is it possible that my papa doesn't love me?" he says to himself. "I saw him kiss my big brother Felix. He threw himself into it, he didn't move away. Why does he avoid me? Does he want to make me jealous? It's always the same. When I'm away from my parents for three months, I'm dying with eagerness to see them. I think I'm going to jump up on them like a puppy and we'll smother each other with kisses. Then I see them and they put the chill on me."

Monsieur Lepic asks him if his Greek isn't doing badly, but deep in his sad thoughts, Poil de Carotte hasn't got the right answers.

POIL DE CAROTTE

It all depends. Greek into French goes better than composition, because in Greek into French you can guess.

MONSIEUR LEPIC

And German?

POIL DE CAROTTE

It's awfully hard to pronounce.

MONSIEUR LEPIC

My word! How are you going to beat the Prussians when war is declared if you don't know their living language?

POIL DE CAROTTE

Oh, I'll know it by that time. You're always threatening me with war. I honestly think the war will wait for me to finish school.

MONSIEUR LEPIC

How did you make out in the last test? You weren't at the tail end, I hope.

POIL DE CAROTTE

Somebody's got to be.

MONSIEUR LEPIC

My word! And I was going to ask you out to lunch. If it were Sunday at least. But on a weekday I really shouldn't interfere with your work.

POIL DE CAROTTE

I personally haven't got much to do; what about you, Felix?

BIG BROTHER FELIX

Only this morning the teacher forgot to give us a written assignment.

MONSIEUR LEPIC

That will leave you more time to learn your lesson.

THE PEN

BIG BROTHER FELIX

Oh, Papa, I know it already. It's the same as yesterday.

MONSIEUR LEPIC

Even so, I think you'd better go back. I'll try to stay till Sunday and we'll make up for lost time.

Neither big brother Felix's pout nor Poil de Carotte's afflicted silence delays the farewells.

Poil de Carotte waits anxiously. "I'll see if I come off any better," he says to himself. "I'll see whether or not my father doesn't like me to kiss him anymore."

And resolutely, head high, he comes closer.

But again, with a defensive gesture, Monsieur Lepic keeps him at a distance.

"One of these days you're going to put my eye out with that pen in your ear. Couldn't you put it somewhere else when you're going to kiss me? Let me point out that I remove my cigarette."

POIL DE CAROTTE

Oh, dear Papa, I'm sorry. It's true, someday something terrible will happen. They've warned me, but my pen is so cozy behind my ear that I leave it there and forget it. I ought to take the point out at least. Oh, my poor dear Papa, I'm glad to know you were scared of my pen.

MONSIEUR LEPIC

My word! You laugh because you almost put my eye out.

POIL DE CAROTTE

No, my dear Papa, I'm laughing about something else: just another silly idea that came into my head.

LES JOUES ROUGES

RED CHEEKS

I

AFTER COMPLETING his usual inspection, the director of the St. Mark's Boarding Establishment leaves the dormitory. Each of the pupils has slipped between the sheets as into a sheath, making himself very small for fear of untucking the covers. Violone, the proctor, casts a look around to make sure that everyone is in bed, and rising on his tiptoes, slowly turns down the gas. Instantly a chattering starts up between neighbors. Whispers criss-cross from bed to bed, lips move, and the dormitory sends up a jumbled murmur in which, now and then, the brief whistling of a consonant is distinguishable.

The sound is muffled, continuous, and in the end irritating. Scurrying invisibly like mice, the babbles seems to be gnawing at the silence.

Violone puts on his slippers, strides up and down for a time between the beds, tickling one pupil's feet, pulling the tassel of another's nightcap, and stops beside Marseau, with whom he regularly chats far into the night. Long after the general conversation has died down, muffled by degrees as though the pupils had gradually pulled their sheets over their mouths, the proctor is still bending over Marseau; resting his elbows heavily on the bedstead, insensible to the paralysis of his forearms and the pins and needles shooting into his fingertips.

He enjoys the boy's childish stories and keeps him awake with intimate secrets and sentimental confessions. From the very start, he has loved this child for his soft, transparent complexion, which seems illumined from within. His skin is so delicate that at the slightest atmospheric change it discloses a network of capillaries comparable to the lines of a map seen through a sheet of tracing paper. Marseau has a delightful way of blushing unexpectedly and for no reason, which attracts people to him as to a girl. Often a schoolmate presses a fingertip to his cheek and suddenly removes it, leaving a white spot. But soon the white gives way to a fine red which spreads quickly like wine in water and covers his whole face from the pink tip of his nose to the lavender of his ears. All are free to do it; Marseau lends himself willingly to these experiments. He has been variously nicknamed Night Light, Lantern, and Red Cheek. He is very much envied for this faculty of blushing at will.

Poil de Carotte, who sleeps in the next bed, is the most envious of all. Skinny and as pale as a Pierrot, pasty-faced, he pinches his bloodless epidermis till it hurts; the result is a dimly pink spot or two, and he can't even count on that. He would gladly gouge stripes in Marseau's scarlet-flushed cheeks with his nails, and peel them like oranges.

His curiosity has been aroused for some time. This evening he starts listening the moment Violone arrives; he is suspicious, perhaps justly so, and determined to discover the truth about the proctor's sneaky ways. An instinctive spy, he brings all his talents to bear, he pretends to snore, rolls over ostentatiously, but always ends up where he started. He lets out a piercing scream as if he were having a nightmare, so that the sleepers start in terror and sheets are buffeted like surf. Then, as soon as Violone has gone, he sits up in bed and hisses at Marseau: "Fag!"

No answer. Poil de Carotte rises on his knees, seizes Marseau by the arm, and shaking him violently: "Do you hear me? Fag!"

Fag doesn't seem to hear him; exasperated, Poil de Carotte goes on: "A fine kettle of fish.... You think I didn't see you. Just try and tell me he didn't kiss you. Try and tell me you're not his fag."

He rises up, stretching his neck like an infuriated white gander, bracing himself on the bed with his fists.

But this time there is an answer:

"Well, what of it?"

With one wriggle Poil de Carotte slips back between the sheets.

The proctor has suddenly reappeared.

II

"Yes," says Violone, "I kissed you, Marseau; you can admit it, you haven't done anything wrong. I kissed you on the forehead, but Poil de Carotte is depraved beyond his years. It was a pure, chaste kiss, a kiss that a father might give his child. But Poil de Carotte doesn't understand that I love you like a son, or a brother if you prefer, and tomorrow the little fool will go around telling everybody heaven knows what."

At these words, spoken in a vibrant undertone, Poil de

Carotte pretends to be asleep. But he raises his head to hear more.

Marseau scarcely breathes as he listens to the supervisor, for though he finds his words perfectly natural, he trembles as though dreading the revelation of some mystery. Violone goes on as softly as he can. Distant, inarticulate words, barely localized syllables. Not daring to turn around, Poil de Carotte wriggles imperceptibly closer, but he can no longer hear anything. He is listening so hard that he feels as if his ears were growing deeper and wider and shaping themselves into funnels, but they catch no sound.

He remembers having sometimes experienced such a sensation of effort when listening at doors, pressing his eye to the keyhole, trying by sheer force of will to make the hole larger and to draw what he wanted to see toward him, as though with a hook. Nevertheless, he would be willing to bet that Violone is repeating: "Yes, my affection is pure, pure, and that's what that little imbecile can't understand."

Finally the proctor bends down as gently as a shadow over Marseau's forehead, kisses it, caresses it with his goatee as with a paintbrush. Then he stands up and goes away. Poil de Carotte follows him with his eyes as he slips between the rows of beds. When Violone's hand grazes a bolster, the disturbed sleeper turns over with a sigh.

Poil de Carotte waits a long while. He is afraid that Violone will suddenly come back again. Marseau is rolled up in a ball, his blanket over his eyes, but wide awake, full of his adventure that he doesn't know what to make of. He sees nothing ugly in it to upset him, and yet in the darkness of his bed Violone's image hovers luminously, as gentle as the visions of women that have aroused him in more than one dream.

Poil de Carotte grows tired of waiting. As though drawn by magnets, his eyelids droop. He forces himself to stare at the feeble gaslight; but after having counted three bursts of little crackling bubbles eager to escape from the jet, he drops off to sleep.

III

The next morning in the washroom, while the corners of napkins, moistened with a little cold water, are lightly rubbed over shivering faces, Poil de Carotte gives Marseau a vicious look, and summoning up a maximum of ferocity, insults him again, hisses through clenched teeth: "Fag! Fag!"

Marseau's cheeks turn almost purple, but he replies without anger and with an almost pleading look: "But I tell you that what you're thinking simply isn't true."

The proctor comes in for hand inspection. Lined up in two rows, the boys mechanically present first the backs, then the palms of their hands, turning them over quickly and immediately putting them back in a warm place, in their pockets or under the nearest quilt. Ordinarily Violone doesn't bother to look at them. This time, ill-advisedly, he decides that Poil de Carotte's hands are not clean. Asked to wash them again, Poil de Carotte rebels. Yes, there's a bluish spot, but he insists that it's the beginning of chillblains. The proctor must have it in for him.

Violone is obliged to take him to the director.

An early riser, the director is sitting in his Empire-green study, preparing for the history class he gives the larger boys. Pressing his stubby fingers to the table cover, he is mapping out the main landmarks: here, the fall of the Roman Empire; in the middle, the Turkish conquest of Constantinople; over here, modern history, which begins no one knows where and never ends.

He is wearing an ample dressing gown; its embroidered braid encircles his powerful chest like cables encircling a mooring mast. Obviously the man eats too much; his features are heavy and always slightly shiny. He speaks in a loud voice even to ladies, and at the top of his collar the folds of his neck undulate slowly and rhythmically. He is also remarkable for the roundness of his eyes and the thickness of his moustache.

Holding his cap between his legs in order to preserve his freedom of action, Poil de Carotte faces the director.

In a terrible voice the director asks, "What is it?"

"The proctor has sent me, Monsieur, to tell you that my hands are dirty, but it's not true."

And again Poil de Carotte conscientiously displays his hands, first the backs, then the palms. And then to clinch it, first the palms and then the backs.

"Ah, so it's not true," says the director. "Four days of restriction, my boy."

"Monsieur," says Poil de Carotte, "the proctor has it in for me."

"Ah, he has it in for you. Eight days, my boy."

Poil de Carotte knows his man and isn't taken aback by his gentle ways. He is determined to go the limit. Taking a resolute pose, he tenses his legs and holds his ground at the risk of a clout on the ear.

For it is one of the director's innocent pastimes to fell a recalcitrant pupil with the back of his hand: bingo. A knowing pupil foresees the blow and ducks; the director is thrown off balance, provoking the stifled laughter of all present. But he doesn't try again, for his dignity forbids him to answer guile with guile. If he can't score a bull's-eye on the selected cheek, he shouldn't have tried.

"Monsieur," says Poil de Carotte, proud of his audacity. "The proctor does things with Marseau."

Instantly the director's eyes cloud over as though two gnats had fallen into them. He sets his two clenched fists on the edge of his desk, half rises, and thrusting his head forward as though to butt Poil de Carotte in the chest, grunts: "What kind of things?"

Poil de Carotte seems taken aback. He was hoping (but better late than never) for a massive volume, by Henri Martin, for instance, hurled by a skillful hand, and here he's being asked for details.

The director is waiting. The folds of his neck merge into a single cushion on which his head sits askew.

Poil de Carotte hesitates, just long enough to convince himself that the words won't come. Then, suddenly discountenanced, his shoulders sagging in what would seem to be an attitude of crestfallen embarrassment, he takes his flattened cap from between his legs and, sagging more and more, raises it slowly to chest height. And with a furtive look, as though shame forbade him to speak, he silently thrusts his apelike head into the padded lining.

IV

The same day, after a brief investigation, Violone is notified of his dismissal. His departure is touching, almost a ceremony.

"A brief absence," says Violone. "I shall be back."

But no one believes him. The Establishment is always changing its staff, as though fearing that mold will set in. Proctors come and go. This one is leaving like the rest, only more quickly because he's nicer. Nearly all the pupils like him. He has no equal for writing titles on notebooks, such as: Greek Exercises. The property of. . . . The capitals are blocked in like the letters in a sign. The children leave their benches and form a circle around his desk. His beautiful hand, set off by a ring with a green gem, moves elegantly over the paper. At the bottom of the page he improvises a signature. Like a stone falling into water, it drops into the waving, eddying

lines of the paraph, a little masterpiece. The tail of the paraph
loses itself in the body. One has to look long and carefully to
find it. The whole, it goes without saying, is done with a single
stroke of the pen. On one occasion he turned out a labyrinth
of lines known as a *cul-de-lampe*, and the children marveled at
it for minutes on end.

His dismissal makes them very sad.

They decide to bumble the director at the first opportunity,
in other words, to puff out their cheeks and imitate bumble-
bees with their lips as a sign of their displeasure. And one fine
day they surely will.

Meanwhile they nurse each other's sadness. Violone, who
knows the boys are sorry to see him go, has the coquetry to
leave during a recreation period. When he appears in the
yard, followed by a hired man carrying his trunk, all the children come running. He shakes hands and strokes faces; sur-
rounded, besieged, smiling and moved, he struggles to free his
coattails without tearing them. Some of the boys stop short in
the middle of a swing on the horizontal bars, and jump to the
ground sweating and breathless, their shirt sleeves rolled up
and their fingers still sticky with rosin. Others, less active,
who are ambling monotonously around the yard, wave good-
bye. Bent beneath the trunk, the hired man has stopped in
order to keep his distance, and a small boy takes advantage of
his immobility to mark his apron with a hand dipped in wet
sand. Marseau's cheeks have flushed so pink as to look painted.
This is his first real sorrow, and faced with the realization that
he is going to miss Violone rather as he might miss a girl
cousin, he stands off to one side, feeling troubled, anxious,
and almost ashamed. Violone is coming toward him without
the slightest embarrassment when a sound of shattering glass
is heard.

All eyes rise to the little barred window of the detention
room. Poil de Carotte's ugly, savage face appears. His hair

over his eyes and his white teeth bared, he grimaces like a pale, vicious little beast in a cage. Sticking his right hand through the broken pane, which bites him like a living creature, he threatens Violone with his bleeding fist.

"You little fool," says the proctor. "Are you happy now?"

"Yes," cries Poil de Carotte, vigorously plunging his fist into another windowpane. "Why did you always kiss him and never me?"

And daubing his face with the blood flowing from the cuts in his hand: "I've got red cheeks too when I want to."

THE LICE

THE MOMENT big brother Felix and Poil de Carotte arrive home from St. Mark's, Madame Lepic makes them take a foot bath. They need it after three months, for at school their feet were never washed. It's not even mentioned in the prospectus.

"I can guess how black yours are, my poor Poil de Carotte!" says Madame Lepic.

She has guessed right. Poil de Carotte's are always blacker than big brother Felix's. One wonders why. The two of them live side by side, doing the same things in the same air. At the end of three months big brother Felix's feet aren't exactly white, but Poil de Carotte's, by his own admission, aren't even recognizable.

Shamed, he plunges them into the water with the dexterity of a prestidigitator. No one sees them emerge from his socks to join big brother Felix's feet which are already at the bottom

[99]

of the tub. Soon the tub is veiled with a layer of grime that conceals the four hideous objects from view.

As usual, Monsieur Lepic strides from window to window. He rereads his sons' term reports, especially the comments written by the principal himself.

Big brother Felix: "Scatterbrained but intelligent. Will succeed." Poil de Carotte: "Distinguishes himself when he wants to, but doesn't always want to."

The family is amused at the idea that Poil de Carotte is sometimes distinguished. At the moment he sits with his arms crossed over his knees, soaking his feet and letting them swell with well-being. He feels that he is being scrutinized. The general opinion is that he has grown uglier under his mop of long, somber-red hair. Monsieur Lepic, who dislikes effusions, shows how glad he is to see him by teasing him. When he goes away, he flips a finger at his ear. When he comes back, he pokes him in the ribs with his elbow, and Poil de Carotte laughs happily.

At length Monsieur Lepic runs his hand through his mane and cracks his nails as though to kill a louse. That is his favorite joke.

And at the very first try he gets one.

"Dead shot," he says. "I never miss."

And while he somewhat disgustedly wipes his fingers on Poil de Carotte's hair, Madame Lepic raises her hands to high heaven.

"I suspected as much," she cries in consternation. "A fine how-do-you-do! Ernestine, go get a basin, we have a job for you."

Ernestine brings a basin, a fine-tooth comb, vinegar and a saucer, and the hunt begins.

"Do me first," cries big brother Felix. "I'm sure he's passed them on to me."

He scrapes his head furiously with his fingernails and asks for a pail of water to drown the bugs in.

"Relax," says sister Ernestine, who takes pleasure in self-sacrifice. "I'm not going to hurt you."

She ties a towel around his neck and proceeds with a mother's skill and patience. Holding his hair to the side with one hand and delicately wielding the comb in the other, she searches without fear of contagion. She doesn't even pout with disdain.

When she says, "One more," big brother Felix stamps his feet in the tub and shakes a fist at Poil de Carotte who is silently waiting his turn.

"That's all for you, Felix," says sister Ernestine. "You only had seven or eight; count them. We'll count Poil de Carotte's too."

At the first stroke of the comb Poil de Carotte takes first place. Sister Ernestine thinks she has struck the nest, but she has only unearthed a random sampling.

The family surrounds Poil de Carotte. Sister Ernestine applies herself. His hands behind his back, Monsieur Lepic looks on like a curious stranger. Madame Lepic emits plaintive cries.

"Oh! Ah!" she exclaims. "We need a shovel and a rake."

Squatting on his heels, big brother Felix moves the basin from place to place and catches the lice. They fall enveloped in dandruff. Their little feet squirm like cut eyelashes. They roll this way and that with the water in the basin, and soon the vinegar kills them.

MADAME LEPIC

Really, Poil de Carotte, I can't understand you anymore. A big boy of your age, you ought to be ashamed of yourself. I forgive your feet, I presume you never see them when you're away from home. But the lice eat you, and you don't breathe a word either to your teachers or your family. Would you explain to us, pray, what pleasure it gives you to let yourself be eaten alive. There's blood in your hair.

POIL DE CAROTTE

It's the comb. It scratches.

MADAME LEPIC

Oh! It's the comb. So that's how you thank your sister. Do you hear him, Ernestine? His lordship is dissatisfied with his hairdresser. My advice to you, child, is to abandon this voluntary martyr to his vermin.

ERNESTINE

I'm through for today, Mama. I've only done the worst of it, I'll give him another going-over tomorrow. But I know someone who's going to wash her hands in cologne.

MADAME LEPIC

As for you, Poil de Carotte, take out your basin and exhibit it on the garden wall. I want the whole village to see it, to your shame.

Poil de Carotte takes the basin and goes out; he puts it in the sun and mounts guard beside it.

The first person to come along is old Marie Nanette. Every time she meets Poil de Carotte, she stops, observes him out of her shrewd little nearsighted eyes, and, wagging her black bonnet, seems to be putting two and two together.

"What's that?" she asks.

Poil de Carotte makes no answer. She leans down over the basin.

"Is it lentils? Goodness, I don't see as well as I used to. My boy Pierre ought to buy me a pair of glasses."

She puts in a finger as though to taste. She just doesn't understand.

"And what are you doing out here, all sulky and bleary-eyed? I bet they've punished you and sent you out of the house. Listen, I'm not your grandma, but I think what I think, I'm sorry for you, poor little fellow, because I have a hunch they make life hard for you."

Poil de Carotte looks around to make sure his mother isn't within hearing. Then he says to Old Nanette:

"What of it? Is it any of your business? Go attend to your own affairs and leave me alone."

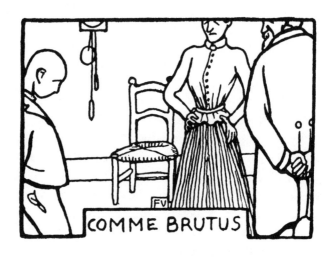

LIKE BRUTUS

MONSIEUR LEPIC

POIL DE CAROTTE, your schoolwork wasn't as good as I had hoped this year. Your reports show that you could do a good deal better. You daydream, you read forbidden books. Thanks to your excellent memory, you learn your lessons well enough, but you neglect your written work. Poil de Carotte, it's time for you to think of buckling down.

POIL DE CAROTTE

You can rely on me, Papa. I admit that I slipped a little this past year. But next year I have every intention of working hard. Of course I can't promise to be first in the class in everything.

MONSIEUR LEPIC

You can try.

POIL DE CAROTTE

No, Papa, you're asking too much. It's not possible in geography or German, or in physics and chemistry. There are two or three jokers who are no good at anything else; they concentrate on those subjects and they're always at the head of the class; they can't be beat. But I've made up my mind—honestly, Papa—to take the lead in French composition and hold it. And if, in spite of all my efforts, I don't succeed, my conscience at least will be clear and I'll be able to cry out with pride like Brutus: O Virtue, thou art only a name!

MONSIEUR LEPIC

Ah, my boy, I think you'll make it.

BIG BROTHER FELIX

What's he saying, Papa?

SISTER ERNESTINE

I didn't catch it.

MADAME LEPIC

Nor I. Please repeat, Poil de Carotte.

POIL DE CAROTTE

Oh nothing, Mama.

MADAME LEPIC

What's that? Red as a beet, shaking your fist at the sky, declaiming loud enough to be heard at the other end of the village, and you weren't saying anything! Repeat that sentence, so we can all benefit.

POIL DE CAROTTE

It's not interesting, Mama.

MADAME LEPIC

Oh yes it is. You were talking about somebody. Whom were you talking about?

POIL DE CAROTTE

Somebody you don't know, Mama.

MADAME LEPIC

All the more reason. Anyway, don't think so much, just do as you're told.

POIL DE CAROTTE

Well, Mama; Papa and I were having a talk, he was giving me some friendly advice, and I don't know what got into me, but somehow I thought I'd show my gratitude by swearing to invoke virtue like a certain Roman called Brutus . . .

MADAME LEPIC

Fiddlesticks! You're floundering. Will you kindly repeat what you said before in the same tone and without changing a word. I'm not asking for the moon and the stars: you can do that much for your mother.

BIG BROTHER FELIX

Would you like me to say it, Mama?

MADAME LEPIC

No, I want him to say it first. Then you can say it and we'll compare. Come along, Poil de Carotte, get a move on.

POIL DE CAROTTE (IN A WHINING STAMMER)

Vi-irt-ue, thou art on-only a name.

MADAME LEPIC

It's hopeless. I can't get a thing out of that child. He'd rather be beaten black and blue than do anything to please his mother.

BIG BROTHER FELIX

Here, Mama, here's how he said it. *(He rolls his eyes and hurls defiant glances.)* If I'm not first in French composition *(He puffs out his cheeks and stamps his foot.)*, I shall cry out like Brutus: *(He raises his arms to heaven.)* O virtue! *(He lets his arms fall, slapping his thighs.)* Thou art only a name! That's the way he said it.

MADAME LEPIC

Bravo, splendid! Congratulations, Poil de Carotte, but an imitation is never as good as the original, and that makes your obstinacy all the more regrettable.

BIG BROTHER FELIX

But Poil de Carotte, was it really Brutus who said that? Wasn't it Cato?

POIL DE CAROTTE

I'm sure it was Brutus. "And then he flung himself on the sword which a friend held out to him and died."

SISTER ERNESTINE

Poil de Carotte is right. I even remember that Brutus pretended to be mad with some gold in a cane.

POIL DE CAROTTE

I beg your pardon, Sister, you're all balled up. You're confusing my Brutus with a different one.

SISTER ERNESTINE

I thought . . . I can assure you that Mademoiselle Sophie is just as good a history teacher as yours.

MADAME LEPIC

It doesn't matter. Don't argue. The main thing is to have a Brutus in the family, to be envied, thanks to Poil de Carotte. We were unaware of our honor. Admire the new Brutus. He talks Latin like a bishop and refuses to repeat the Mass for the deaf. Turn him around: in front you see spots on a jacket that he's wearing today for the first time; in back you see a rip in his breeches. Heavens above, what has he got into now? Friends, take a good look at Poil de Carotte Brutus! Pooh, you nasty little brute!

SELECTED LETTERS

*from Poil de Carotte to Monsieur Lepic
and a few replies
from Monsieur Lepic to Poil de Carotte*

POIL DE CAROTTE TO MONSIEUR LEPIC

The St. Mark's Boarding Establishment

MY DEAR PAPA,

My fishing expeditions during vacation stirred up my blood and now I have big boils on my leg. I am in bed. I lie on my back and the nurse puts on poultices. The boils hurt until they come to a head. Then I forget about them. But they multiply like little chickens. For each one cured I get three more. But I hope it won't be anything serious.

YOUR AFFECTIONATE SON

POIL DE CAROTTE

My dear Poil de Carotte,

Since you are preparing for your first communion and learning your catechism, you must be aware that you are not the first member of the human race to suffer. Jesus Christ had nails in his hands and feet. Nails are worse than boils, yet he didn't complain.

Chin up!

YOUR LOVING FATHER

POIL DE CAROTTE TO MONSIEUR LEPIC

My dear Papa,

It gives me pleasure to announce that I have a new tooth. Though I'm not old enough, I think it must be a precocious wisdom tooth. I venture to hope that it will not be the only one and that you will always be pleased with my good conduct and application.

YOUR AFFECTIONATE SON

MONSIEUR LEPIC'S ANSWER

My dear Poil de Carotte,

Just as your tooth was emerging, one of mine began to wobble. It finally came out yesterday morning. In consequence, you possess one tooth the more and your father one the less. Thus nothing has changed and the number of teeth in the family remains unchanged.

YOUR LOVING FATHER

POIL DE CAROTTE TO MONSIEUR LEPIC

My dear Papa,

Just imagine, yesterday Monsieur Jâques, our Latin teacher had his birthday, and the class unanimously chose me to present their best wishes. Flattered at the honor, I spent a long time composing a speech, which I larded with Latin quotations for the occasion. False modesty aside, I was quite pleased with it. I made a clean copy on a large sheet of paper. When the day came, my classmates egged me on—"Go on, don't be afraid"—and taking advantage of a moment when Monsieur Jâques was looking the other way, I stood up and walked toward his desk. But no sooner had I unrolled my scroll and begun to declaim in a loud voice:

REVERED MASTER

than Monsieur Jâques rose in a fury and shouted:

"Will you kindly get back to your seat this very minute!"

As you may well imagine, I returned to my seat without delay while my friends hid behind their books and Monsieur Jaques angrily told me to translate the lesson for the day.

My dear Papa, what do you think of that?

MONSIEUR LEPIC'S REPLY

My dear Poil de Carotte,

When you are a deputy, you'll see worse. Each man to his role. If the authorities have made Monsieur Jâques a teacher, it is no doubt because they wished him to make speeches, not listen to yours.

POIL DE CAROTTE TO MONSIEUR LEPIC

MY DEAR PAPA,

I have just given your hare to Monsieur Legris, our history and geography teacher. He seemed definitely pleased at the gift and sends you his heartfelt thanks. When I went in with my wet umbrella, he took it from me and put it in the vestibule. Then we talked of one thing and another. He told me that if I wished I ought to carry off first prize in history and geography at the end of the year. But would you believe that I remained standing throughout our conversation and that Monsieur Legris, who, I repeat, was perfectly amiable in other respects, did not even offer me a chair?

Was it absentmindedness or rudeness?

I cannot imagine. I should be curious, my dear Papa, to know your opinion.

MONSIEUR LEPIC'S ANSWER

MY DEAR POIL DE CAROTTE,

You are always complaining. You complain because Monsieur Jâques tells you to be seated and because Monsieur Legris leaves you standing. Perhaps you are too young to expect to be treated with consideration. And if Monsieur Legris failed to offer you a chair, forgive him: perhaps he was deceived by your small stature and thought you were already seated.

POIL DE CAROTTE TO MONSIEUR LEPIC

MY DEAR PAPA,

I hear you are going to Paris. I share the pleasure you will have at visiting the capital which I too should like to see, and where I shall be with you in spirit. I am well aware that my schoolwork stands in the way of such a trip, but avail myself of the opportunity to ask you if you might buy me one or two books. I know my own by heart. Select any you please. When you come right down to it, one is as good as another. But what I should especially like is the *Henriade* by François-Marie-Arouet de Voltaire, and the *Nouvelle Héloïse* by Jean-Jacques Rousseau. If you bring them back for me (books cost nothing in Paris), you may be sure that the proctor will never confiscate them.

MONSIEUR LEPIC'S ANSWER

MY DEAR POIL DE CAROTTE,

The writers you speak of were men like you and me. What they did, you can do. Write books, you can read them afterward.

MONSIEUR LEPIC TO POIL DE CAROTTE

MY DEAR POIL DE CAROTTE,

The letter I received from you this morning amazes me no end. I have reread it, to no avail. It is not in your usual style and you speak of weird things which, it seems to me, are beyond your ken and mine.

Ordinarily you tell us about your daily life, your marks, the good and bad qualities you find in your teachers, the names of your new friends, the state of your underwear, the food, and whether you have slept well.

That interests me, but this letter leaves me baffled. Why, if you please, this excursion into the springtime in midwinter? What are you driving at? Do you need a muffler? Your letter is not dated and there is no way of knowing whether it is addressed to me or to the dog. Even your handwriting seems changed, and the disposition of the lines and the profusion of capitals are disconcerting. In short, you seem to be making fun of someone, yourself I presume. I am not finding fault, only giving you my impressions.

POIL DE CAROTTE'S ANSWER

MY DEAR PAPA,

A line in haste to explain my last letter. You didn't notice that it was *in verse.*

LE TOITON

THE REFUGE

THE LITTLE HOUSE where chickens, rabbits and pigs have lived by turns is empty now. In vacation time it is Poil de Carotte's private property. It's easy to get in, for the door is gone. The threshold is graced by a few spindly nettle plants which, when Poil de Carotte lies on his belly, look to him like a forest. The ground is covered by fine dust. The stones of the wall glisten with moisture. Poil de Carotte's hair grazes the roof. Here he is at home. Disdainful of cumbersome toys, he relies on his imagination for distraction.

His chief amusement is to dig four nests with his rear end, one in each corner. Using his hands for a trowel, he builds up cushions of dust, and wedges himself in.

His back to the smooth wall, his hands crossed over his bent knees, he feels sheltered and happy. He couldn't possibly make himself smaller. He forgets the world, loses all fear of it. It would take a good thunderclap to upset him.

Puffs of coolness come to him from the dishwater that runs down nearby, sometimes in torrents, sometimes drop by drop, through the hole in the sink.

A sudden alert.

Approaching cries. Steps.

"Poil de Carotte? Poil de Carotte?"

A head is lowered. Rolled up tight, pushing himself into the ground and the wall, openmouthed, unbreathing, his very eyes immobilized, Poil de Carotte senses that someone is searching the half darkness.

"Poil de Carotte, are you there?"

His temples pound, he is in agony. He almost cries out in anguish.

"The little wretch isn't there. Where in the devil can he be?"

The steps retreat and Poil de Carotte's body expands a little, makes itself more comfortable.

His thoughts explore long roads of silence.

But then a din fills his ears. Under the roof a fly, caught in a spiderweb, struggles and buzzes. And the spider glides along a thread. Its belly has the whiteness of bread. For an instant it remains suspended, contracted, anxious.

Poil de Carotte waits, on tenterhooks, anticipating the outcome. And when the tragic spider charges, closes the star of its legs, and hugs its prey, he stands up avidly as though he wanted his share.

Nothing more.

The spider climbs back to its place. Poil de Carotte sits down again, crawls back into himself, into the darkness of his frightened animal's soul.

Soon like a trickle of water blocked by sand, his daydream stops for lack of impetus, forms a puddle and stagnates.

LE CHAT

THE CAT

I

POIL DE CAROTTE has heard that for crayfish bait nothing, neither chicken innards nor butcher's scraps, can equal cat meat.

And it so happens that he knows a cat, despised because he is old, sick, and partly bald. Poil de Carotte invites him into his refuge for a cup of milk. They will be alone. Conceivably a rat could venture out of the wall, but Poil de Carotte promises only a cup of milk. He has set it in a corner. He pushes the cat over to it and says, "Have yourself a feast."

He strokes his back, calls him affectionate names, watches the swift lapping of the tongue, and is moved to pity.

"Poor old fellow, it's your last meal. Enjoy it."

The cat empties the cup, cleans the bottom, wipes the edge, and has only his sweetened lips left to lick.

"Finished? Really finished?" asks Poil de Carotte, still caressing the cat. "You'd probably like another cup; but that's all I was able to steal. And besides, a little sooner, a little later . . ."

At these words he sets the barrel of his carbine to the cat's forehead and fires.

The report stuns Poil de Carotte. He thinks the whole hut has blown up. When the cloud clears, he sees the cat at his feet, looking at him out of one eye.

Half the head is gone and blood is flowing into the milk cup.

"He doesn't look dead," says Poil de Carotte. "Damn it, my aim was right."

The eye has a yellowish gleam. Poil de Carotte is too frightened to stir.

The cat's trembling indicates that he is alive, but he makes no attempt to move. He seems to be bleeding into the cup on purpose, taking care not to waste a drop.

Poil de Carotte is no beginner. He has killed wild birds, domestic animals, a dog, for his own pleasure or at the behest of others. He knows how it's done, he knows that if an animal doesn't want to die, you've got to be quick, work yourself into a lather, and if necessary risk close combat. If you don't, you're in for an attack of squeamishness. You lose your nerve. You waste time; you never get it over with.

First he attempts a few cautious jabs. Then he seizes the cat by the tail and hits him in the neck with his gun stock, so violently that each blow would seem to be the coup de grace.

The dying cat claws the air wildly, rolls up in a ball and unrolls without a whimper.

"Who was it told me that cats cry when they die?" says Poil de Carotte.

He grows impatient. It's taking too long. He throws down

the carbine and picks up the cat in his arms. Excited by the claws in his flesh, his blood on fire, he clenches his teeth and smothers him.

But he has smothered himself too. Utterly exhausted, he staggers and falls, and there he sits, his face pressed to the cat's face, his two eyes peering into the cat's eye.

II

Poil de Carotte is lying on his iron bed.

Bent beneath the low roof of the former henhouse, his parents and their friends, who have been sent for in haste, visit the scene of the tragedy.

"Ah!" says his mother. "Believe me, it took all my strength and then some to get that mangled cat away from him. I can assure you, he doesn't hug me like that."

And while she describes an act of ferocity which, retold in later years by the family fireside, will take on legendary proportions, Poil de Carotte sleeps and dreams.

He is walking by the side of a brook in which the rays of an inevitable moon move this way and that, crisscrossing like knitting needles.

The pieces of cat in his crayfish nets shine through the transparent water.

The meadow is lined with white mists, perhaps concealing tenuous ghosts.

Poil de Carotte keeps his hands behind his back to show the ghosts that they have nothing to fear.

An ox approaches, and stops, panting. Then it runs off, filling the sky with the sound of its four hooves, and vanishes.

How peaceful it would be if the talkative brook didn't keep babbling, whispering, chattering like a gathering of old women.

As though to bludgeon the brook into silence, Poil de Carotte raises one of his net handles, but just then swarms of giant crayfish emerge from the rushes.

They grow still larger and rise out of the water, erect and glittering.

Weighed down with fear, Poil de Carotte is unable to run away.

And the crayfish surround him.

They climb up toward his throat.

Their joints crackle.

They open wide their claws.

LES MOUTONS

THE SHEEP

AT FIRST Poil de Carotte sees nothing but dim, round, jumping objects. They emit deafening, intermingled cries like children playing in a school yard. One of them tumbles against his legs and for a moment he is frightened. Another leaps full into the beam of light cast by the overhead window. It's a lamb. Poil de Carotte smiles to think he was afraid. Growing accustomed to the darkness, he begins to see things in detail.

The lambing season has set in. Every morning farmer Pajol counts two or three new lambs. He finds them scattered among the mothers, tottering awkwardly on their stiff legs: four crudely sculptured sticks.

Poil de Carotte is still afraid to pat them. Bolder than he, they nibble at his shoes or, sucking at a wisp of hay, climb up on him with their forepaws.

The veterans, already a week old, leap with a violent effort of their haunches and zigzag through the air. The skinny day-old ones fall on their angular knees and get up again, bursting with life. Sticky and not yet licked, a little one, just born, drags himself over the ground. Encumbered by her swaying, water-swollen pouch, the mother pushes the lamb away with little thrusts of her head.

"A bad mother," says Poil de Carotte.

"Animals are like people," says Pajol.

"She'd probably like to put it out to nurse."

"Looks like it," says Pajol. "We have to put some of them on the bottle. It doesn't last. The mothers take pity. Besides, we know how to bring them around."

He takes the mother by the shoulders and shuts her up in a cage by herself. He ties on a straw necktie to recognize her by if she gets out. The lamb has followed her. The ewe eats with a sound like a grater, and shivering, plaintive, its muzzle enveloped in trembling jelly, the lamb lifts itself on shaky limbs and tries to suck.

"And you think she'll develop more human feelings?" Poil de Carotte asks.

"Yes, when her hind end has healed: she had a hard delivery."

"I still think I'm right," says Poil de Carotte. "Why not hand the baby over to a wet nurse for a while?"

"She wouldn't have him."

He is not mistaken. From end to end of the stable the mothers' bleats intermingle, sounding the dinner hour, and though all sound the same to Poil de Carotte, the lambs know which is which, for without the least confusion each one runs straight to its mother's teats.

"No baby snatchers around here," says Pajol.

"Amazing," says Poil de Carotte, "All that family instinct in a ball of wool. How do you account for it? Maybe it's their acute sense of smell."

He almost wants to stop up one of the lambs' noses to see.

Drawing profound comparisons between men and sheep, he asks to know the lambs' names.

While the little ones suck avidly, their mothers, their flanks assailed by abrupt thrusts of the nose, eat peacefully, indifferently.

Poil de Carotte looks into a watering trough and sees pieces of chain, fragments of wheel rim, a discarded shovel.

"That's a fine watering trough," he says with mild irony. "I suppose the iron builds up their blood."

"Exactly," says Pajol. "You take pills, don't you?"

He invites Poil de Carotte to taste the water. He tosses in everything he can think of to make it more tonic.

"Would you like a tick?" Pajol asks.

"Sure," says Poil de Carotte though he isn't so sure. "Thanks in advance."

Pajol runs his fingers through the thick wool of a mother sheep and catches a plump, yellow, glutted tick between his nails. According to Pajol, two ticks of that size would devour a child's head like a plum. He lays it in the hollow of Poil de Carotte's hand and suggests that if he wants a good laugh he should put it on his brother's or sister's neck, or in their hair.

The tick is already at work on Poil de Carotte's skin. He feels a tingling in his fingertips as though sleet were falling on them, then on his wrist and elbow. The tick seems to be everywhere, gnawing at his arm all the way up to the elbow.

"It can't be helped," says Poil de Carotte to himself. He crushes it and wipes his fingers on a sheep's back while Pajol isn't looking.

He'll say he lost it.

For a moment Poil de Carotte listens thoughtfully to the bleating, which gradually dies down. Soon there is no other sound than the muffled crunch of hay being ground by slow-moving jaws.

Hanging from a bar of the crib, a lone overcoat with faded stripes seems to be guarding the sheep.

PARRAIN

GODFATHER

SOMETIMES Madame Lepic lets Poil de Carotte visit his godfather and even spend the night. He is a gruff, solitary old man who spends his time fishing or working in his vineyard. He cares for no one, tolerating only Poil de Carotte.

"So there you are, duckling," he says.

"Yes, Godfather," says Poil de Carotte without kissing him. "Have you got my fishing line ready?"

"One will do for both of us," says Godfather.

Poil de Carotte opens the barn door and sees that his line is ready. His godfather always teases him this way, but Poil de Carotte is used to it and doesn't mind it anymore. It's one of the old man's eccentricities and it doesn't interfere with their good relations. When he says Yes, he means No and vice versa. You only have to remember which is which.

"If it amuses him, what do I care," thinks Poil de Carotte.

And they remain good friends.

[124]

In Poil de Carotte's honor, Godfather, who ordinarily cooks only once a week, puts a big pot of beans on the fire with a good chunk of salt pork in them, and to start the day right makes him drink a glass of uncut wine.

Then they go fishing.

Godfather sits down by the shore and methodically unrolls his silk gut. He weights his imposing lines with heavy stones and catches only big fish, which he swaddles in a towel like babies, and deposits in the shade.

"The main thing," he tells Poil de Carotte, "is not to pull up your line until your floater has gone down three times."

POIL DE CAROTTE

Why three times?

GODFATHER

The first doesn't mean a thing: the fish is nibbling. The second time is serious: he's swallowing. The third time, it's sure. He won't get away. You can never pull up too late.

Poil de Carotte likes best to fish for gudgeon. He takes off his shoes, wades into the river, and stirs up the sandy bottom with his feet. The stupid gudgeon come running, and Poil de Carotte catches one every time he throws out his line. He barely has time to cry out: "Sixteen, seventeen, eighteen! . . ."

When Godfather sees the sun overhead, they go home for lunch. He stuffs Poil de Carotte full of white beans.

"There's nothing I like better," he says, "but they have to be cooked to a mash. I'd sooner bite into a pickax than eat a bean that crunches under your teeth like a ball of shot in a partridge wing."

POIL DE CAROTTE

These melt in your mouth. Usually Mama makes them

pretty well. But not like this. She probably economizes on cream.

GODFATHER

Duckling, it's a pleasure to see you eat. I'll bet you don't eat your fill at your mother's.

POIL DE CAROTTE

It all depends on her appetite. If she's hungry, I eat her fill. When she serves herself, she serves me too. When she's finished, I've finished too.

GODFATHER

You can ask for more, stupid.

POIL DE CAROTTE

That's easy for you to say, old-timer. Anyway, it's healthier not to be full.

GODFATHER

To think that I have no children. Why, I'd lick a monkey's rear end if it was my child. Try and make sense out of that.

They end their day in the vineyard. Poil de Carotte follows his godfather around and watches him dig. The rest of the time, he lies on a pile of cut vine shoots, sucking blades of osier.

THE SPRING

IF HE SPENDS the night with his godfather, it's not for the
good sleeping. The room is cold, but the feather bed is too
hot; a comfort to the godfather's old bones, it soon bathes the
godchild in sweat. But at least he is away from his mother.

"Does she frighten you as much as that?" says Godfather.

POIL DE CAROTTE

Or you could say that I don't frighten her enough. When
she wants to punish my brother, he grabs a broomstick and
stands up to her, and believe me, she stops short. She prefers
to appeal to his finer feelings. She says Felix has such a sensitive nature lickings are no use, but my nature is just right for
them.

GODFATHER

You ought to try the broom, Poil de Carotte.

POIL DE CAROTTE

Ah, if only I dared! Felix and I often fight, for fun or for real. I'm as strong as he is. I could defend myself as well as he does. But I can see myself standing up to Mama with a broom. She'd think I'd gone to get it for her. It would pass from my hands into hers, and maybe she'd even say thank you before starting in.

GODFATHER

Sleep, duckling, sleep.

Neither of them can sleep. Suffocating, gasping for air, Poil de Carotte tosses and turns, and his old godfather feels sorry for him.

Suddenly, just as Poil de Carotte is dozing off, Godfather grabs him by the arm.

"Are you there, duckling? I was dreaming. I thought you were still in the spring. Do you remember the spring?"

POIL DE CAROTTE

As if I was in it. I don't want to complain, but you talk about it quite a lot.

GODFATHER

Poor duckling, whenever I think of it, I tremble all over. I'd fallen asleep in the grass. You were playing by the spring, you slipped, you fell, you yelled, you struggled, and I, like a miserable no-good, I didn't hear a thing. There was hardly enough water to drown a cat. But you didn't stand up. That was the trouble. Didn't you think of standing up?

POIL DE CAROTTE

How can you expect me to remember what I thought about when I was in the spring?

GODFATHER

Finally you woke me with your splashing. It was high time. Poor duckling! Poor duckling! You threw up water like a pump. We changed your clothes, we gave you little Bernard's Sunday suit.

POIL DE CAROTTE

Yes, it prickled. I couldn't help scratching. It must have been made out of horsehair.

GODFATHER

No, but little Bernard didn't have a clean shirt to lend you. I can laugh about it now, but in another minute, another second, I'd have picked you up dead.

POIL DE CAROTTE

I'd be far away from . . .

GODFATHER

Hush. I cursed myself good and proper, and I haven't had a good night's sleep since. Sleepless nights, that's been my punishment. I deserved it.

POIL DE CAROTTE

But I don't deserve it, Godfather, and now I want to sleep.

GODFATHER

Sleep, duckling, sleep.

POIL DE CAROTTE

If you want me to sleep, Godfather, let go my hand. I'll give it back to you when I wake up. And take your leg away too, it's hairy. I can't sleep with anybody touching me.

THE PLUMS

FOR A TIME they toss restlessly under the feather bed, and
Godfather says, "Duckling, are you asleep?"

POIL DE CAROTTE

No, Godfather.

GODFATHER

Neither am I. I feel like getting up. If you like, we'll go
looking for worms.

"Good idea," says Poil de Carotte.

They jump out of bed, dress, light a lantern, and go out
into the garden.

Poil de Carotte carries the lantern, and Godfather a tin
box half full of wet earth. That's where he keeps his supply of
worms. He covers them with wet moss and always has some

in reserve. When it has rained all day, the pickings are good.

"Be careful not to step on them," he says to Poil de Carotte. "Step lightly. If I weren't afraid of catching cold, I'd wear slippers. At the slightest sound, they crawl back into their holes. You can only catch a worm when he goes too far from home. You've got to grab him suddenly and squeeze a little so he can't squirm out. If he's half in the ground, let him go: you'd only break him and a broken worm is no good. In the first place, he rots the others, and besides the fish won't touch him. Some fishermen try to save on worms; that's a mistake. You can only catch good fish with a whole live worm that curls up in the water. The fish thinks he's trying to get away, chases him, and swallows him unsuspecting."

"Most of them get away from me," mutters Poil de Carotte. "And my fingers are all full of their dirty slime."

GODFATHER

A worm isn't dirty. A worm is the cleanest thing you'll ever come across. All they eat is soil, and when you squeeze them all they spit up is soil. I'd be willing to eat them.

POIL DE CAROTTE

You can have my share. Let's see you eat one.

GODFATHER

These here are kind of fat. You'd have to roast them and spread them on bread. But I eat the little ones raw, the ones you find in prunes, for instance.

POIL DE CAROTTE

Yes, I know. And you give my family the creeps, especially Mama; just thinking about you makes her sick to her stomach. As for me, I wouldn't imitate you but I approve of you, because you're not hard to please and we get along fine.

He raises his lantern, draws the branch of a plum tree toward him and picks a few plums. He keeps the good ones and gives the wormy ones to Godfather, who swallows them, pit and all, saying: "They're the best."

POIL DE CAROTTE

I'll take to it one of these days, I'll eat them the same as you. But now I'm afraid I'd smell bad and Mama would notice it if she kissed me.

"They don't smell," says Godfather, and he blows in his god-son's face.

POIL DE CAROTTE

That's a fact. You don't smell of anything but tobacco. But you sure stink of that. I like you fine, my good old godfather, but I'd love you even more, more than anybody else, if you didn't smoke a pipe.

GODFATHER

Duckling, duckling! It makes a man live longer.

MATHILDE

SISTER ERNESTINE is out of breath. "Do you know what, Mama?" she says to Madame Lepic, "Poil de Carotte is playing husband and wife again with little Mathilde in the meadow. Big brother Felix is dressing them. It's forbidden if I'm not mistaken."

And sure enough, out in the meadow, little Mathilde is standing stiff as a poker under her bridal veil of white-flowering birthwort. In full regalia, she truly resembles a bride adorned with orange blossoms. And there's enough birthwort on her to still all the labor pains in the world.

Braided into a wreath on her head, it descends in waves under her chin, behind her back, along her arms, twines about her waist, and reaching the ground forms a train to which the indefatigable Felix is still adding.

Finally, he steps back and says, "Don't move. Now it's your turn, Poil de Carotte."

And he proceeds to dress Poil de Carotte as a young bridegroom, covering him too with birthwort, but mixing in a few poppies, haws, and a dandelion, to make him distinguishable from Mathilde. It doesn't occur to Poil de Carotte to laugh, and all three of them keep a straight face. They know the right tone for every ceremony. At funerals you must be sad from beginning to end, at marriages you've got to be solemn until after Mass. Or else there's no fun in playing.

"Join hands," says big brother Felix. "Now comes the procession. Not too fast."

At a dignified distance from one another, they advance slowly. When Mathilde gets tangled in her train, she lifts it up and holds it between her fingers. One foot still raised, Poil de Carotte gallantly waits for her.

Big brother Felix guides them about the meadow. He walks backward, marking the cadence with his outstretched arms. He is the mayor greeting them, the priest blessing them, then a friend who congratulates them, and then, scraping one stick over another, the violinist.

He walks them back and forth.

"Stop," he says. "It's coming undone."

He clouts Mathilde's wreath back into place, and immediately starts the procession off again.

"Ouch," says Mathilde with a grimace.

A tendril of birthwort is pulling her hair. Big brother Felix pulls off the whole train. The game continues.

"That's that," he finally says. "Now you're married. Now you smooch."

They hesitate. "Well, what are you waiting for? Do something. A little courtship. A declaration of love. You look like a couple of dummies."

With an air of superiority, he, who may already have uttered words of love, makes fun of their helplessness. And setting an example, he kisses Mathilde first.

Poil de Carotte plucks up courage, finds Mathilde's face behind the creepers, and kisses her on the cheek.

"I mean it," he says. "I'd marry you in a minute."

As willingly as she received it, Mathilde returns his kiss. Suddenly embarrassed, both of them stand blushing.

Big brother Felix taps his forehead.

"You're both blushing like tomatoes."

He rubs one forefinger over the other, stamps his feet, and drools at the mouth.

"Are they dumb! They think they're married for real."

"In the first place," says Poil de Carotte, "I'm not blushing at all. Go ahead and laugh, it'll take more than you to prevent me from marrying Mathilde if Mama's willing."

But here comes Mama to announce in person that she's not willing. She pushes the gate. She steps into the meadow, followed by Ernestine, the tattletale. Passing beside the hedge, she breaks off a switch; she strips the leaves but leaves the thorns.

She heads straight for them, as inexorable as a storm.

"Trouble!" says big brother Felix.

He runs off to the end of the meadow, where he can watch in safety.

Poil de Carotte never runs away. Though cowardly by nature, he usually prefers to get it over with; and today he feels brave.

All a-tremble, Mathilde weeps and sobs like a widow.

POIL DE CAROTTE

Don't be afraid. I know Mama. She's only out for me. I'll catch it all.

MATHILDE

Yes, but your mama will tell my mama, and my mama will give me a licking.

POIL DE CAROTTE

A correction, that's the right word. They correct us like homework. Does your mother correct you?

MATHILDE

Sometimes; it all depends.

POIL DE CAROTTE

With me it's a sure thing.

MATHILDE

But I haven't done anything.

POIL DE CAROTTE

That doesn't make any difference. Watch out!

Madame Lepic is approaching. She's got them where she wants them, she has plenty of time. She slows down. She is so close that sister Ernestine, for fear of blows on the rebound, stops at the edge of the circle where the action will take place. Poil de Carotte takes a stance in front of "his wife," who is sobbing harder than ever. The white blossoms of the birthwort mingle. Madame Lepic's switch rises, ready to swoop. Livid, Poil de Carotte crosses his arms and pulls in his neck. He feels the heat in his loins, his calves sting in advance. And he has the gumption to cry out:

"What difference does it make as long as we have a good time?"

LE COFFRE-FORT

THE SAFE

THE NEXT DAY Poil de Carotte meets Mathilde, and she reports: "Your mother came over and told my mother all about it, and she gave me a good spanking. How about you?"

POIL DE CAROTTE

Me? I don't remember. But you didn't deserve a spanking; we weren't doing anything wrong.

MATHILDE

No, of course we weren't.

POIL DE CAROTTE

I meant it when I said I'd be glad to marry you.

MATHILDE

I'd be glad to marry you too.

POIL DE CAROTTE

You might think I look down on you because you're poor and I'm rich, but I don't, I respect you.

MATHILDE

How rich are you, Poil de Carotte?

POIL DE CAROTTE

My parents have at least a million.

MATHILDE

How much is a million?

POIL DE CAROTTE

Plenty; millionaires have so much money they can never spend it all.

MATHILDE

My parents are always complaining about not having any.

POIL DE CAROTTE

Oh, mine do that too. They all do. They all want to make people feel sorry for them instead of being jealous. But I know we're rich. On the first of the month Papa goes to his room alone. I hear the lock of the safe squeaking. It sounds like the tree frogs in the evening. Papa says a word nobody knows, neither Mama nor my brother nor my sister, nobody but him and me, and the door of the safe opens. Papa takes out money and puts it on the kitchen table. He doesn't say a thing, he just jingles the coins so that if Mama's busy at the stove, she'll know they're there. It happens every month, and it's been going on for ages. Which proves there's more than a million in the safe.

MATHILDE

And to open it he says a word. What word?

POIL DE CAROTTE

Don't try to guess, you'd be wasting your time. I'll tell you when we're married if you promise never to repeat it.

MATHILDE

Tell me now. I promise I'll never repeat it.

POIL DE CAROTTE

No, it's a secret between Papa and me.

MATHILDE

You don't know it. If you knew it, you'd tell me.

POIL DE CAROTTE

I know it all right.

MATHILDE

You do not. You do not. And it serves you right.

"You want to bet?" says Poil de Carotte solemnly.

"Bet what?" asks Mathilde, weakening.

"Let me touch you wherever I want," says Poil de Carotte, "and I'll tell you the word."

Mathilde looks at Poil de Carotte. She doesn't exactly understand. She half closes her gray, scheming eyes, and now she has two subjects of curiosity instead of one.

"First tell me the word, Poil de Carotte."

POIL DE CAROTTE

You swear you'll let me touch you wherever I want?

MATHILDE

Mama doesn't allow me to swear.

POIL DE CAROTTE

Then I won't tell you the word.

MATHILDE

Who cares? I've guessed it. That's right, I've guessed it.

Losing patience, Poil de Carotte tries to force matters. "Listen Mathilde, you haven't guessed anything at all. But your word of honor is good enough for me. The word Papa says before opening his safe is Squidgillum. Now I can touch you wherever I want."

"Squidgillum! Squidgillum!" says Mathilde, torn between the pleasure of knowing a secret and the fear that it doesn't amount to a row of pins. "You're sure you're not making fun of me?"

Then as Poil de Carotte, without answering, steps forward, resolutely holding out his hand, she runs away. And Poil de Carotte hears her shrill laughter.

She disappears, and he hears somebody snickering behind him.

He turns around. One of the hired hands of the manor is looking out of the stable window, showing his teeth.

"I saw you, Poil de Carotte," he cries out. "And I'm going to tell your mother all about it."

POIL DE CAROTTE

Good old Pierre, I was only playing. Trying to put one over on the little girl. Squidgillum is a fake name, I made it up. I don't even know the real one.

PIERRE

Never mind that, Poil de Carotte. I don't give a hoot about Squidgillum and I won't tell your mother about that. But I'll tell her the rest.

POIL DE CAROTTE

What rest?

PIERRE

The rest. I saw you, I saw you, Poil de Carotte; just try and say I didn't. You're stepping pretty lively for your age. But wait till you get home. Your jug handles won't ever be the same.

Poil de Carotte finds no answer. So red in the face that the natural color of his hair seems to pale, he walks away sniveling, with his hands in his pockets and his tail between his legs.

LES TÉTARDS

THE TADPOLES

POIL DE CAROTTE is playing in the yard, keeping to the middle so that Madame Lepic can watch him from the window. He is doing his best to play "nicely" when his friend Rémy turns up. Rémy is a boy his own age, who limps and always wants to run, with the result that his left leg, the bad one, drags behind the other and can never catch up. He is carrying a basket and says: "Coming, Poil de Carotte? Papa's putting the hemp in the river. We'll help him and we'll catch tadpoles in the baskets."

"Ask my mother," says Poil de Carotte.

RÉMY

Why me?

POIL DE CAROTTE

Because if I ask her, she won't let me.

[143]

Just then Madame Lepic shows her face in the window.

"Madame," says Rémy. "Please, may I take Poil de Carotte to catch tadpoles?"

Madame Lepic puts her ear to the pane. Rémy repeats, this time shouting. Madame Lepic has understood. Her lips are seen to move. The two friends hear nothing and exchange questioning looks. But Madame Lepic shakes her head. It's unmistakably no.

"She doesn't want me to go," says Poil de Carotte. "I guess she's going to need me later."

RÉMY

Too bad. We'd have had a good time. But if she won't let you, she won't let you.

POIL DE CAROTTE

Don't go. We can play here.

RÉMY

Nothing doing. I'd rather fish for tadpoles. It's a nice warm day. I'll get whole basketfuls.

POIL DE CAROTTE

Wait a while. Mama always says no to begin with. But sometimes she changes her mind.

RÉMY

I'll wait ten minutes. But no more.

They stand there with their hands in their pockets, furtively watching the stairs, and soon Poil de Carotte pokes Rémy with his elbow.

Sure enough, the door opens and Madame Lepic comes

out, carrying a basket for Poil de Carotte. Then a suspicious look comes over her face and she stops on the first step.

"What's this, Rémy? You still here? I thought you'd gone. I'm going to tell your father you've been dawdling; he'll give you a good scolding.

RÉMY

Poil de Carotte told me to wait.

MADAME LEPIC

Oh! Is that so, Poil de Carotte?

Poil de Carotte doesn't say Yes and he doesn't say No. He doesn't remember. He knows Madame Lepic like a book. Once again he had figured her right. But now that this idiotic Rémy has put his foot in it and spoiled everything, Poil de Carotte knows what's going to happen and loses interest. He crushes a clump of grass underfoot and looks away.

"That's funny," says Madame Lepic. "I wouldn't say I was in the habit of changing my mind."

She adds nothing and returns up the stairs. She goes back into the house with the basket which Poil de Carotte was to have taken, and which she had expressly emptied of fresh walnuts.

By this time Rémy is far away.

Madame Lepic doesn't do things by halves. Other people's children approach her with the utmost caution and are almost as much afraid of her as they are of the schoolmaster.

Rémy heads for the river, galloping so fast that his left foot, always in the lag, dances and clanks like a saucepan and leaves a line in the dust of the road.

His day wasted, Poil de Carotte gives up trying to play.

A promising afternoon has been spoiled.

Regrets are on their way.

He's waiting for them.

Alone and defenseless, he makes no attempt to ward off boredom, the worst punishment of all.

COUP DE THEATRE

COUP DE THÉÂTRE

SCENE I

MADAME LEPIC

WHERE are you going?

POIL DE CAROTTE
(He has put on his new tie and spat on his shoes till they are wringing wet.)

I'm going for a walk with Papa.

MADAME LEPIC

I forbid you to go, do you hear? You'd better obey me, or else . . . *(Her right hand moves back as though winding up.)*

POIL DE CAROTTE
(in a hushed tone)

I see.

SCENE II

POIL DE CAROTTE

(meditating beside the clock)

What is my aim in life? To avoid whacks. Papa gives me fewer than Mama. I've figured it out. And he's the loser.

SCENE III

MONSIEUR LEPIC

(He loves Poil de Carotte but is always gadding about the country on business trips and neglects him.)

Come along. Let's go.

POIL DE CAROTTE

No, Papa.

MONSIEUR LEPIC

What do you mean, no? Don't you want to come?

POIL DE CAROTTE

Of course I do, but I can't.

MONSIEUR LEPIC

Explain yourself. What's wrong?

POIL DE CAROTTE

Nothing, but I'm not going.

MONSIEUR LEPIC

Here we go again! Another one of your whims. What a funny little animal you are! There's no knowing which ear to

[148]

pull you by. You want to go, you don't want to go. Stay home then and snivel at your ease.

SCENE IV

MADAME LEPIC
(*always careful to listen behind doors*)

Poor darling! (*She runs her hand affectionately through his hair and pulls it.*) Crying his eyes out because his father . . . (*with a mean look at Monsieur Lepic*) . . . wants to take him out against his will. Your mother would never torment you so.
(*Monsieur and Madame Lepic turn their backs on one another.*)

SCENE V

POIL DE CAROTTE
(*Deep in the cupboard; in his mouth two fingers, in his nose one finger.*)

Everybody can't be an orphan.

EN CHASSE

HUNTING

MONSIEUR LEPIC takes his sons hunting by turns. They walk behind him, slightly to the right to keep out of the way of his gun, and carry the game bag. Monsieur Lepic is an indefatigable walker. Poil de Carotte follows him with passion and perseverance, and never complains. His shoes chafe, his fingers cramp, he doesn't say a word; his big toes swell up at the ends, which gives them the shape of small hammers.

When Monsieur Lepic shoots a hare early in the day, he says, "Should we leave it at the first farm or hide it in a hedge, and pick it up on the way back?"

"No, Papa," says Poil de Carotte. "I'd rather carry it."

Sometimes he carries two hares and five partridges all day. He slips his hand or his handkerchief under the strap of the game bag to rest his aching shoulder. If they meet someone, he displays his back with ostentation and for a moment forgets his burden.

But he is tired, especially when they bag no game and his vanity ceases to buoy him up.

Occasionally Monsieur Lepic says, "Wait for me here while I beat that field."

Exasperated, Poil de Carotte stands waiting in the sun. He watches his father trampling the field, furrow by furrow, clod by clod, smoothing it down like a harrow, beating hedges, bushes, clumps of thistle with his gun, while even Pyramus is so fagged out that he makes for the shade and lies down for a moment, panting, his tongue hanging out.

"But there's nothing there," thinks Poil de Carotte. "Go ahead, beat, rummage, knock down the nettles. If I were a hare holed up in the leaves at the bottom of a ditch, I certainly wouldn't think of moving in this heat."

And under his breath, he calls Monsieur Lepic mildly insulting names.

Monsieur Lepic jumps another fence to beat the alfalfa in the next field, where he'd be very much surprised not to raise a hare.

"He tells me to wait for him," Poil de Carotte mutters, "and now I've got to run after him. A day that begins badly is sure to end badly. Wear yourself out, exhaust the dog, break my back. We might just as well be sitting down. There won't be anything to show for our pains."

For Poil de Carotte is naively superstitious.

Every time he touches the peak of his cap, Pyramus points, his coat bristling, his tail bolt upright. Monsieur Lepic tiptoes as close as possible, his gun nestling in the hollow of his shoulder. Poil de Carotte stops still, gagging with emotion.

He raises his cap.

Partridges flush or a hare starts from cover. And depending on whether Poil de Carotte *lets his cap fall back into place or goes through the motions of an elaborate greeting,* Monsieur Lepic misses or hits.

Poil de Carotte admits that his system isn't infallible. If repeated too often, his trick doesn't work, as though fortune grew bored with responding to the same signs. Poil de Carotte spaces his maneuver carefully, and then it is almost always successful.

"Did you see that shot?" asks Monsieur Lepic, picking up a hare and pressing its blond belly so as to empty its bowels for the last time. "Why are you laughing?"

"Because you got him on account of me," says Poil de Carotte.

And proud of his latest triumph, he confidently expounds his method.

"Are you serious?" Monsieur Lepic asks.

POIL DE CAROTTE

Well, I wouldn't go so far as to say that I never go wrong.

MONSIEUR LEPIC

Will you kindly be still, you little fool. You're supposed to be a bright boy. If you want to keep your reputation, I wouldn't advise you to trot out such blarney in front of strangers. They'd laugh in your face. Unless, by chance, you're pulling your father's leg.

POIL DE CAROTTE

Oh no, Papa, certainly not. But you're right, forgive me, I'm nothing but a blockhead.

LA MOUCHE

THE FLY

THE HUNT CONTINUES, and Poil de Carotte, who feels so stupid that his shoulders are stooped over with remorse, follows his father with renewed zeal, careful to set his left foot exactly where Monsieur Lepic has set his left foot, and stretching his legs as though running away from an ogre. He stops only to grab a blackberry, a wild pear, or a handful of sloeberries, which pucker the mouth, whiten the teeth, and appease thirst. And in one of the pockets of the game bag there is also a flask of brandy. Nip by nip, he drinks nearly all of it, for Monsieur Lepic, intoxicated by the hunt, forgets to ask for any.

"Care for a drop, Papa?"

A negative sound is borne on the wind. Poil de Carotte takes the drop for himself, empties the flask, and with spinning head starts off again in pursuit of his father. Suddenly he

stops, plunges a finger into his ear and wiggles it vigorously; he pulls it out, pretends to be trying to listen, and shouts:
"Papa, I think there's a fly in my ear."

MONSIEUR LEPIC

Take it out, Son.

POIL DE CAROTTE

It's too far in, I can't get at it. I hear it buzzing.

MONSIEUR LEPIC

It'll die all by itself.

POIL DE CAROTTE

But suppose it lays eggs, Papa, and makes a nest?

MONSIEUR LEPIC

Try to kill it with a corner of your handkerchief.

POIL DE CAROTTE

Suppose I poured in some brandy to drown it? May I?

"Pour in anything you like," cries Monsieur Lepic. "Only make it fast."

Poil de Carotte applies the bottle to his ear and empties it a second time in case Monsieur Lepic should decide to ask for his share.

And soon Poil de Carotte cries out joyfully as he runs:

"Papa, you know what, I don't hear the fly anymore. It must be dead. Only it drank up all the brandy."

LA PREMIÈRE BÉCASSE

THE FIRST WOODCOCK

"STAND THERE," says Monsieur Lepic. "It's the best place. I'll go through the woods with the dog; we'll flush the woodcocks, and when you hear *pit, pit,* prick up your ears and keep your eyes open. They'll be overhead."

Poil de Carotte holds the gun cradled in his arms. It's his first chance at woodcock. He has already shot a quail, taken some feathers off a partridge, and missed a hare with Monsieur Lepic's gun.

He had shot the quail on the ground, under the nose of the pointing dog. At first he had looked at the little earth-colored ball without seeing it.

"Move back," said Monsieur Lepic, "you're too close."

But instinctively Poil de Carotte had taken a step forward, raised his gun and fired point-blank, driving the little gray ball into the ground. All he found of his mangled quail was a few feathers and a bloody beak.

But what really establishes a young hunter's reputation is a woodcock, and Poil de Carotte wants this afternoon to mark an event in his life.

Dusk, as everyone knows, is deceptive. The outlines of things grow blurred and unstable. The sound of a mosquito becomes almost as alarming as the approach of thunder. Poil de Carotte is as nervous as a cat and wishes he had this moment behind him.

Thrushes returning from the fields dart swiftly between the oak trees. He takes aim at them to practice his eye. He rubs the mist off the gun barrel with his sleeve. Here and there a dried leaf scurries.

At last two woodcocks, heavy fliers because of their long beaks, rise into the air and chase one another lovingly, spiraling over the rustling trees.

They go *pit, pit* as Monsieur Lepic promised, but so feebly that Poil de Carotte doubts they are coming his way. His eyes dart here and there. He sees two shadows passing over his head and, his gun stock against his belly, fires in their general direction.

One of the two birds falls beak forward, and the echo carries the deafening report to the four corners of the forest.

Poil de Carotte picks up the woodcock, whose wing is broken, brandishes it with pride, and breathes in the smell of the powder.

Pyramus comes running, followed at a distance by Monsieur Lepic, who is in neither more nor less of a hurry than usual.

"He won't believe his eyes," thinks Poil de Carotte, anticipating praises.

But Monsieur Lepic parts the branches, emerges, and says in an even voice to his son who is still drunk on powder smoke:

"Why on earth didn't you get them both?"

L'HAMEÇON.

THE FISH HOOK

POIL DE CAROTTE is scaling fish, gudgeon, ablet, and even a few perch. He scrapes them with a knife, splits them open, pops the transparent double bladders under his heel, and gathers up the entrails for the cat. Absorbed, working as fast as he can, he is leaning over the bucket of frothy-white water, taking care not to get wet.

Madame Lepic comes over to have a look.

"Not bad," she says. "That's a nice mess of fish you've caught us. You're not so clumsy when you try."

She pats him on the neck and shoulders, but as she is taking her hand away, she cries out in pain.

A fish hook is stuck in the tip of her finger.

Sister Ernestine comes running. Big brother Felix follows, and soon Monsieur Lepic himself is on the scene.

"Let's see it," they say.

But she buries her finger in her skirt, squeezes it between

her knees, and the hook digs deeper. While big brother Felix and sister Ernestine hold her, Monsieur Lepic takes her arm and lifts it. Now everyone can see her finger. The hook has passed right through.

Monsieur Lepic tries to take it out.

"Oh no! Not like that!" cries Madame Lepic.

The hook is stopped at one end by its barb and at the other by the eye.

Monsieur Lepic puts on his glasses.

"Confound it," he says. "We'll have to break the hook."

But how? Monsieur Lepic can't get a proper hold on it. And every time he moves it, Madame Lepic writhes and screams. Do they want to tear the heart and life out of her? To make matters worse, the fish hook is of well-tempered steel.

"In that case," says Monsieur Lepic, "we'll have to cut into the flesh."

He settles his glasses and takes out his penknife. First he presses the dull blade to the finger so feebly that it fails to penetrate. He presses harder; he is sweating. Blood appears.

"Oh! Oh! Oh!" cries Madame Lepic, and the whole group trembles.

"Quicker, Papa," says sister Ernestine.

"Take it easy," says big brother Felix to his mother.

Monsieur Lepic loses patience. The penknife saws and slashes every which way. "You butcher," Madame Lepic gasps. And then fortunately, she faints.

Monsieur Lepic seizes the opportunity. Livid and frantic, he hacks and bores, reducing her finger to a bloody mash from which the fish hook falls.

Oof!

Poil de Carotte has been no help at all. At his mother's first cry, he had run away. Sitting on the stairs with his head in his hands, he tries to figure out what went wrong. The hook must have got stuck in his back when he was casting his line.

"Now I see why the fish didn't bite," he says to himself.

He listens to his mother's cries, at first without dismay. Soon it will be his turn to yell, every bit as loud, as loud as he can. He'll yell himself hoarse to make her think she's sufficiently avenged and decide to lay off.

"What's wrong, Poil de Carotte?"

He doesn't answer. He stops his ears and his red head disappears. The neighbors line up at the foot of the stairs, waiting for news.

Finally Madame Lepic appears. She is as pale as a newly delivered mother and, proud to have been in great danger, she exhibits her carefully swaddled finger. Fighting down a last vestige of pain, she smiles at the neighbors, reassures them in a few words, and says gently to Poil de Carotte:

"You've put me through the mill, my darling. Oh, I'm not angry with you. It wasn't your fault."

Never has she taken this tone with Poil de Carotte. He raises his head in stupefaction. He sees his mother's finger wrapped in rags and string, clean, fat and square like a poor child's doll. His dry eyes fill with tears.

Madame Lepic bends down. As usual, he ducks behind his elbow. But magnanimous, she kisses him in front of all the neighbors.

He doesn't understand. The tears stream down his face.

"But I've told you it's forgotten, I forgive you. What a horror you must think I am."

Poil de Carotte is shaken with sobs.

"What a silly child! You'd think he was being skinned alive," says Madame Lepic. And the neighbors are touched by her kindness.

She hands them the fish hook, which they examine with

curiosity. One of them points out that it's a Number 8. Little by little, she recovers her eloquence and volubly describes the incident.

"Ah, at the time I'd have killed him if I didn't love him so much. What a nasty little gadget! I thought it was going to carry me off to heaven."

Sister Ernestine suggests that they bury it at the far end of the garden, and stamp on the ground.

"Oh no," says big brother Felix. "I'm going to keep it. I'm going to fish with it. Boy, a fish hook soaked in Mama's blood, that will be something. Wait and see the fish I catch, boy oh boy, as big as a house."

And he shakes Poil de Carotte, who, still amazed at having escaped punishment, exaggerates his contrition, heaving raucous sighs and bathing the freckles of his homely, much-slapped face in an unchecked flood.

LA PIÈCE D'ARGENT

THE SILVER PIECE

I

MADAME LEPIC

HAVEN'T YOU lost something, Poil de Carotte?

POIL DE CAROTTE

No, Mama.

MADAME LEPIC

Why are you in such a hurry to say No? Turn out your pockets first.

POIL DE CAROTTE

(He pulls out his pockets and gapes at them. They hang down like a donkey's ears.)

Oh yes, Mama. Give it back to me.

MADAME LEPIC

Give back what? Then you have lost something? I was only guessing. What have you lost?

POIL DE CAROTTE

I don't know.

MADAME LEPIC

Be careful. You're going to tell a lie. You're starting to flounder like a stunned perch. Answer me slowly. What have you lost? Your top?

POIL DE CAROTTE

That's it. I'd forgotten. Yes, Mama, it's my top.

MADAME LEPIC

No, Mama. It's not your top. I confiscated it last week.

POIL DE CAROTTE

Then it's my knife.

MADAME LEPIC

What knife? Who gave you a knife?

POIL DE CAROTTE

Nobody.

MADAME LEPIC

My poor child, you're getting in deeper and deeper. You act as if you were afraid of me. Goodness, we're all alone. I'm questioning you as gently as can be. A son who loves his mother tells her everything. I'm willing to bet you've lost your silver piece. I don't know a thing, mind you, but I'm sure of it. Don't deny it. Your nose is wiggling.

POIL DE CAROTTE

It was my silver piece, Mama. My godfather gave it to me on Sunday. I've lost it, that's my hard luck. It's too bad, but I'll get over it. Actually it didn't mean a thing to me. It was only a coin!

MADAME LEPIC

Is that so, my little orator! And I, poor woman, stand here and listen to you. So it means nothing to you that your godfather will feel badly? That he'll be furious.

POIL DE CAROTTE

Let's imagine I spent my coin on something that appealed to me. Was I just supposed to look at it for the rest of my life?

MADAME LEPIC

That's enough of your poppycock. You had no right to lose that coin or to squander it without permission. It's gone; replace it, find it, make it, do something. Run along and stop arguing.

POIL DE CAROTTE

Yes, Mama.

MADAME LEPIC

And I forbid you to say "yes, Mama" and put on airs; the Lord help you if I hear you humming and whistling between your teeth, playing the carefree vagabond. That doesn't go down with me.

II

Sighing, Poil de Carotte takes little mincing steps along the garden paths. He looks a little and sniffles a good deal. When he feels that his mother is watching him, he stands still or bends down and gropes through the sorrel or the fine sand with his fingers. When he thinks Madame Lepic has gone, he stops looking. He keeps walking as a matter of form, with his nose in the air.

Where in the devil can that coin be? Up there in the tree, in some old nest?

Sometimes people who aren't looking for anything find gold pieces. It's been known to happen. Poil de Carotte could crawl on the ground and wear out his knees and ankles without finding so much as a pin.

Sick of wandering around hoping for heaven knows what, Poil de Carotte gives up and decides to go back in, to gauge his mother's humor. Maybe she has calmed down and is ready to forget about this silver piece that refuses to be found.

No sign of Madame Lepic. Timidly, he calls her.

"Mama! Oh, Mama!"

No answer. She has just gone out. The drawer of her sewing table is open. In among the wool, the needles, the white, red and black spools, Poil de Carotte spies a few silver pieces.

They seem to be growing old in the drawer, sleeping, seldom awakened, pushed from corner to corner, mixed up and unnumbered.

There might be three of them, or there might be as many as four or eight. It would be hard to count them, you'd have to turn the drawer upside down and shake the balls of wool. There would be no way of proving anything.

With the presence of mind that abandons him only on

great occasions, Poil de Carotte resolutely thrusts out his arm, takes one of the coins, and runs away.

Fear of being surprised saves him from hesitation or remorse. It would be dangerous to go back to the sewing table now, and the idea doesn't even enter his head.

He goes straight out, too wound-up to stop, explores the garden paths, chooses his place, and "loses" the silver piece. He grinds it into the ground with his heel and lies down on his belly. The grass tickles his nose. He crawls about, describing irregular circles like a blindfolded child revolving around the hidden object while the player who has done the hiding claps his hands and cries out: "You're getting warm. Careful, it's going to burn you."

III

POIL DE CAROTTE

Mama, I've got it.

MADAME LEPIC

So have I.

POIL DE CAROTTE

What? Here it is.

MADAME LEPIC

Here it is.

POIL DE CAROTTE

My goodness! Show me.

MADAME LEPIC

You show me.

POIL DE CAROTTE

> *(He shows his silver piece.* Madame Lepic *shows
> hers.* Poil de Carotte *feels them, compares them,
> and prepares his speech.)*

That's funny. Where did you find it? I found it on this path, at the foot of the pear tree. I must have walked over it a dozen times before I saw it. It glistened. At first I thought it was a piece of paper or a white violet. I was afraid to pick it up. It must have fallen out of my pocket one day when I was cavorting in the grass. Bend down, Mama, see the place where the sneaky thing was hiding. It can pride itself on having given me plenty of worry.

MADAME LEPIC

Maybe so.

I found it in your other topcoat. In spite of everything I say, you still forget to empty your pockets when you change clothes. I wanted to teach you a lesson. I let you look to teach you to be orderly. But it seems that he who seeks will always find, for now you have two silver pieces instead of one. You're rolling in wealth, my boy. All's well that ends well, but a word of warning: Money is not the source of happiness.

POIL DE CAROTTE

Then I can go and play?

MADAME LEPIC

I should think so. Enjoy yourself, you'll never be any younger. Take your two silver pieces.

POIL DE CAROTTE

Oh, Mama, one is enough. In fact I wish you would keep it for me until I need it. Won't you, please?

MADAME LEPIC

Borrow or lend, lose a friend. Keep your silver pieces. They both belong to you, your godfather's and the one from under the pear tree, unless its owner comes to claim it. Who could it be? I'm racking my brains. Have you any idea?

POIL DE CAROTTE

No, I really haven't, and I don't much care; I'll think about it tomorrow. See you soon, Mama, and thank you.

MADAME LEPIC

Wait! Suppose it was the gardener?

POIL DE CAROTTE

Would you like me to run over and ask him?

MADAME LEPIC

No, angel, stay here and help me. Let's think. We could hardly suspect your father of negligence at his age. Your sister puts her savings in her money box. Your brother hasn't time to lose money, it melts away in his hands.

Come to think of it, maybe *I* lost it.

POIL DE CAROTTE

I can't believe that, Mama. You're so neat and orderly.

MADAME LEPIC

Grown-ups can make mistakes too. I'll have a look. In any case, it concerns no one but myself. Let's not talk about it anymore. Stop worrying, child, run and play, not too far away, while I take a look into the drawer of my sewing table.

(Poil de Carotte, who was already running off to play, turns around. For a moment he trails after

his mother. Then suddenly he passes her, turns, stands in her path, and silently holds out his cheek.)

MADAME LEPIC
   (raising her right hand, threatening devastation)

I knew you were a liar, but not as bad as all that. Now you're telling double lies. You can look forward to a bright future. Anybody who steals a mouse will steal a house, and end up murdering his mother.
   (The first whack descends.)

LES IDÉES PERSONNELLES

HIS OWN IDEAS

Monsieur Lepic, big brother Felix, sister Ernestine and Poil de Carotte are sitting around the fireplace, in which a stump is burning, roots and all. The four chairs are rocking on their front legs. A discussion is in progress. Taking advantage of Madame Lepic's absence, Poil de Carotte expounds his own ideas.

"To me," he says, "family ties mean nothing. You, Papa, for instance, you know how I love you. But I don't love you because you're my father; I love you because you're my friend. The fact is, I see no merit in your being my father, but I regard your friendship as a great favor which you don't owe me, but generously accord me.

"Ah!" says Monsieur Lepic.

"And what about me? And me?" say big brother Felix and sister Ernestine.

"Same thing," says Poil de Carotte. "Chance has made you

my brother and sister. Why should I be grateful to you for that? Is it any fault of ours that all three of us are Lepics? You had no way of preventing it. Have I any reason to thank you for being involuntarily related to me? I thank you only, you, my brother, for your protection, and you, my sister, for your tender care."

"At your service," says big brother Felix.

"Where does he get these unearthly ideas?" asks sister Ernestine.

"And," Poil de Carotte adds, "there's nothing personal about what I am saying. I mean it in the most general sense. If Mama were here, I'd repeat it in her presence."

"You wouldn't repeat it twice," says big brother Felix.

"What harm do you see in what I've said?" says Poil de Carotte. "Don't misinterpret my ideas. I am not lacking in sentiment. I love you more than I seem to. But instead of being commonplace, dictated by instinct and habit, my affection is deliberate, rational . . . logical. Yes, logical, that's the word I was looking for."

"When will you get over the habit of using words whose meaning escapes you?" says Monsieur Lepic, getting up to go to bed, "and of delivering lectures at your age? If I had treated your late grandfather to a quarter of the applesauce you dish out, he'd have given me a good boot in the tail to show me that I was still his boy and nothing more."

"I was only talking to pass the time," says Poil de Carotte, beginning to feel uneasy in his mind.

"You'd do better to keep still," says Monsieur Lepic, candle in hand.

And he disappears. Big brother Felix follows him.

"See you around, old pal," he says to Poil de Carotte.

Sister Ernestine stands up and says gravely:

"Good evening, sir."

Poil de Carotte is left to his perplexity.

Only yesterday Monsieur Lepic advised him to learn to think: "Why do you keep saying: 'they say.'? Who's 'they'? There's no such animal. Everybody is nobody. You're too much inclined to reel off things you've heard. Try to think for yourself a little. Express your own ideas, even if you have only one for a starter."

And now his first attempt at an idea of his own has met with a very cool reception. Poil de Carotte banks the fire, lines up the chairs along the wall, says good night to the clock, and withdraws to his room, which is reached by the cellar stairs and known as the cellar room. It's a cool room, pleasant in the summertime. Game hung there keeps at least a week. Blood is dripping into a dish from the nose of the most recent hare. There are baskets full of grain for the chickens, and Poil de Carotte never wearies of plunging in his arms up to the elbow and stirring the feed about.

The whole family's clothes are hanging on the rack. Ordinarily they give him a spooky feeling. They suggest a row of suicides who have been careful to line up their shoes on the top shelf before hanging themselves.

But tonight Poil de Carotte is not afraid. He doesn't look under the bed. Neither the moon nor the shadows frighten him, nor the well in the garden, that seems to have been put there expressly in case somebody felt like jumping into it from this very window.

He would be afraid if he thought of being afraid, but that's all over now. In his nightgown, he forgets to walk on his heels so as to keep the soles of his feet off the cold red tiles.

And lying in bed, staring at the blisters in the wet plaster, he continues to develop his "own ideas," so called because it's best to keep them to yourself.

LA TEMPÊTE DE FEUILLES

THE TEMPEST OF LEAVES

For a long time now, Poil de Carotte has been watching the highest leaf of the big poplar tree.

He stands there in a daydream, waiting for it to move.

Solitary, detached from the tree, stemless and free, it seems to have a life of its own.

Every day it catches the first and last rays of sun.

Since noon it has been deathly still, more like a spot than a leaf, and Poil de Carotte has lost patience. He feels uneasy when finally it gives a sign.

Below it a nearby leaf gives the same sign. Others repeat it, communicate it to nearby leaves, which quickly pass it on.

It's a sign of alarm, for the hem of a brown cloak has appeared on the horizon.

Already the poplar is shivering, trying to move, to drive away the mass of sultry air which is making it uncomfortable.

Its restlessness infects the beech, an oak, the chestnut trees, and all the trees in the garden make signs to tell each other that the cloak is widening in the sky, that its clear dark border is approaching.

First they wave their slender branches, silencing the birds, the blackbird which had been tossing out a note now and then like a pebble, the painted turtledove which only a moment ago Poil de Carotte heard cooing by fits and starts, the insufferable magpie, and the swallow with its swallowtail.

Then they set their great tentacles in motion to frighten the enemy.

The livid invading cloak comes slowly closer.

Little by little it arches over the sky. It pushes back the blue, plugs up the holes that might admit air, and prepares to smother Poil de Carotte. Sometimes it seems about to collapse under its own weight and fall down on the village; but for fear of being torn, it stops at the tip of the steeple.

Now it is so close that, without further provocation, panic and tumult set in.

The trees intermingle their hazy angry forms, in the midst of which Poil de Carotte imagines nests full of round eyes and white beaks. The leaves fly away in companies, but return in a fright and try to fasten on again. The sensitive acacia leaves sigh; those of the scarred birch sing a plaint; the chestnut leaves whistle, and the twining Dutchman's pipe clatters as its vines chase each other over the wall.

Lower down, the squat apple trees shake off their apples which strike the ground with muffled blows.

Still lower, the red currant bushes shed drops of blood and the black currants drops of ink.

Lower still, the cabbages drunkenly shake their ass's ears, and overgrown onions clash together, bursting their swollen seedpods.

Why? What has got into them? And what does all this mean? It's not thundering. It's not hailing. Not a flash of lightning nor a drop of rain. It's that stormy blackness up there, that silent night in midday that has driven them wild and filled Poil de Carotte with terror.

Now the entire cloak has unfolded beneath the masked sun.

It's moving, Poil de Carotte knows that; composed of shifting clouds, it will glide away; he will see the sun again. Yet, though it covers the whole sky, it squeezes his head, his forehead. He closes his eyes and it presses painfully against his eyelids.

He puts his fingers in his ears too. But the storm invades him with its cries and its whirlwind.

It picks up his heart like a scrap of paper in the street.

And crumples it, and rolls it up small.

Poil de Carotte's heart is nothing but a little ball.

LA RÉVOLTE

REVOLT

I

MADAME LEPIC

Poil de Carotte, angel, would you please be so sweet as to bring me a pound of butter from the mill. Hurry. We won't sit down to table without you.

POIL DE CAROTTE

No, Mama.

MADAME LEPIC

Why do you say: No, Mama? Of course we'll wait for you.

POIL DE CAROTTE

No, Mama, I won't go to the mill.

MADAME LEPIC

What's that? You won't go to the mill? What's that you're saying? Who's asking you? . . . Are you dreaming?

POIL DE CAROTTE

No, Mama.

MADAME LEPIC

See here, Poil de Carotte, I don't understand. I order you to go to the mill this instant and bring back a pound of butter.

POIL DE CAROTTE

I heard you. I won't go.

MADAME LEPIC

Then *I* must be dreaming? What's going on? Are you refusing to obey me for the first time in your life?

POIL DE CAROTTE

Yes, Mama.

MADAME LEPIC

You refuse to obey your mother?

POIL DE CAROTTE

Yes, Mama. I refuse to obey my mother.

MADAME LEPIC

I can't believe it. Will you run along?

POIL DE CAROTTE

No, Mama.

MADAME LEPIC

Will you kindly be still and run along?

POIL DE CAROTTE

I'll be still, but I won't run along.

MADAME LEPIC

Will you take this dish and run along?

II

Poil de Carotte says nothing and doesn't budge.

"It's a revolution!" cries Madame Lepic on the stairs, raising her arms to high heaven.

And indeed, it's the first time Poil de Carotte has ever said No to her. If at least she had disturbed him! If he had been playing! But he'd been sitting on the ground, twiddling his thumbs and sniffing at the breeze, with his eyes closed to keep them warm. And now he's looking her square in the face. She simply can't understand. She cries out, as though for help.

"Ernestine, Felix, something has happened. Come here. Bring your father and Agathe too. There can't be too many of you."

And even the rare passersby are free to stop in.

Poil de Carotte is standing in the middle of the yard, keeping his distance, surprised at his firmness in the presence of danger, and even more surprised that Madame Lepic has forgotten to beat him. The situation is so dreadful that her weapons fail her. She forgets her usual gestures of intimidation, forgets to narrow her eyes into an instrument as sharp and terrifying as the tip of a red-hot poker. But her lips part under the pressure of her inner fury, which escapes with the sound of hissing steam.

"Ah, friends," she says. "I politely asked Poil de Carotte to do me a little favor, to stop off at the mill as long as he was going for a walk. Try and guess what he said. Ask him, or you'd think I was making it up."

They have no trouble guessing, and Poil de Carotte's defiant attitude makes speech on his part superfluous.

Gentle Ernestine comes over and whispers in his ear, "Watch your step. You're heading for trouble. Do as you're told. Take your loving sister's advice."

Big brother Felix is enjoying the show. He wouldn't give up his seat for a fortune. It doesn't even occur to him that if Poil de Carotte starts shirking, his elder brother will come in for a share of the errands; on the contrary, he's all for him. Yesterday he despised him as a namby-pamby. Today he respects him as an equal. Big brother Felix is enjoying himself thoroughly.

"It's the end of the world upside-down," says Madame Lepic, utterly crushed. "I wash my hands of it. Let somebody else try to tame the vicious beast. I choose to retire. It's a matter to be settled between father and son. I wish you luck."

"Papa," says Poil de Carotte. He hasn't got into the swing of it yet, and his voice is choked with emotion. "If you tell me to go to the mill for a pound of butter, Papa, I'll go, but only for you. I refuse to go for my mother."

Monsieur Lepic seems more dismayed than flattered at being thus preferred. It embarrasses him to exert his authority under pressure from the gallery—and all over a pound of butter.

Ill at ease, he takes a few steps in the grass, shrugs his shoulders, turns his back, and goes back into the house.

For the present, the matter ends there.

LE MOT DE LA FIN

THE LAST WORD

MADAME LEPIC is absent from dinner; she has taken to her bed. All sit silent, partly from habit, but partly out of embarrassment. After the last mouthful Monsieur Lepic knots his napkin, tosses it on the table, and says:

"Doesn't anybody feel like taking a walk with me as far as the shanty on the old road?"

Poil de Carotte understands that this is an invitation. He stands up, takes his chair over to the wall as usual, and meekly follows his father.

At first they walk along in silence. The inevitable question is slow in coming. In his mind, Poil de Carotte practices guessing what it will be and answering. He is ready. Though shaken, he regrets nothing. He has already been through such a storm of emotion, he has no fear of anything worse. At length Monsieur Lepic makes up his mind, and at the mere sound of his voice, Poil de Carotte is reassured.

MONSIEUR LEPIC

I am waiting for an explanation of your conduct. You have made your mother very unhappy.

POIL DE CAROTTE

My dear Papa, I've been hesitating a long time, but it's time I admitted it. All right: I don't love Mama anymore.

MONSIEUR LEPIC

Ah! For what reason? And since when?

POIL DE CAROTTE

Every reason. Since I've known her.

MONSIEUR LEPIC

Ah, that's too bad, my boy. Tell me at least what she's done to you.

POIL DE CAROTTE

That would be a long story. But don't you notice anything?

MONSIEUR LEPIC

Yes, I've noticed that you sulk quite a lot.

POIL DE CAROTTE

It exasperates me when people say that I sulk. "Of course Poil de Carotte can't be seriously angry. He's only sulking. Leave him alone. When he's had enough, he'll come out of his corner, calm and smiling. Most of all, don't seem to take an interest. It's unimportant."

Forgive me, Papa, but it's unimportant only for the father and mother and strangers. I do sulk now and then, I admit, as a matter of form, but there are times, I assure you, when something makes me really and truly angry and I never forget it.

MONSIEUR LEPIC

Nonsense; pinpricks. You'll forget the whole thing.

POIL DE CAROTTE

No, no. You just don't realize; you're at home so little.

MONSIEUR LEPIC

I'm obliged to travel.

POIL DE CAROTTE (*self-important*)

I know, Papa, business is business. You have other fish to
fry, but Mama has literally nothing to fry but me. I wouldn't
dream of blaming you. Of course I could tattletale, you'd pro-
tect me. Now that you've asked me, I'll tell you about the past
little by little. You'll see whether I'm exaggerating and
whether I have a long memory. But, Papa, I wish you would
give me some advice right now.

I should like to be separated from my mother.

What would be the simplest way, in your opinion?

MONSIEUR LEPIC

You only see her two months a year, at vacation time.

POIL DE CAROTTE

You ought to let me spend my vacation at school. It would
help my studies.

MONSIEUR LEPIC

That is a privilege reserved for poor pupils. People would
think I had abandoned you. And besides, you're thinking only
of yourself. What about me? I'd miss your company.

POIL DE CAROTTE

You'd come and see me, Papa.

MONSIEUR LEPIC

Pleasure trips are expensive, Poil de Carotte.

POIL DE CAROTTE

You'd take advantage of your business trips. You'd make a little detour.

MONSIEUR LEPIC

No. I've always treated you like your brother and sister, taking care to favor none of you. I shall continue to do so.

POIL DE CAROTTE

Then let's drop my studies. Take me out of school on the pretext that I'm wasting your money, and I'll choose a trade.

MONSIEUR LEPIC

What trade? Do you want me to apprentice you to a shoemaker, for instance?

POIL DE CAROTTE

It makes no difference what. I'd earn my living and I'd be free.

MONSIEUR LEPIC

It's too late, my poor Poil de Carotte. If I've made sacrifices to give you an education, it's not to have you mending shoes.

POIL DE CAROTTE

But, Papa, what if I told you that I've tried to kill myself?

MONSIEUR LEPIC

You're overdoing it, Poil de Carotte.

POIL DE CAROTTE

I swear that only yesterday I tried to hang myself.

MONSIEUR LEPIC

And here you are. Which proves that you didn't really want to. But you're mighty proud of yourself over an unsuccessful try. You imagine that no one else has ever been tempted by death. Poil de Carotte, egoism will be your ruin. You think only of yourself. You think there's nobody else in the world.

POIL DE CAROTTE

Papa, my brother is happy, my sister is happy, and if, as you say, Mama takes no pleasure in tormenting me, I give up. As for you, you're a strong man, people are afraid to tread on your toes, even my mother wouldn't dare to. She can't prevent you from being happy. Which proves that there are happy people in the human race.

MONSIEUR LEPIC

Human race, my foot. My poor boy, you're talking through your hat. Can you see into people's hearts? Do you understand everything?

POIL DE CAROTTE

Everything that concerns me, yes, Papa; at least I try.

MONSIEUR LEPIC

In that case, Poil de Carotte, forget about being happy. I warn you, you'll never be happier than you are now, never, never.

POIL DE CAROTTE

That's encouraging.

MONSIEUR LEPIC

Resign yourself. Harden yourself until you come of age, then you'll be your own master. Then you can run off and leave us; you'll be free to change your family, if not your character and disposition. Meanwhile, try to control yourself, stifle your sensibility, and observe others, the members of your family for instance. It will amuse you. I can promise you some comforting surprises.

POIL DE CAROTTE

I know other people have their troubles. But I'll feel sorry for them another day. Today I demand justice for myself. Just tell me who isn't better off than I am. I have a mother. This mother of mine doesn't love me, and I don't love her.

"And what about me? Do you suppose I love her?" says Monsieur Lepic with sudden impatience.

At these words Poil de Carotte lifts his eyes to his father. For a long while he scrutinizes his hard face, his thick beard, into which his mouth has withdrawn as though ashamed of having said too much, his creased forehead, his crow's-feet, and his drooping eyelids that make him seem to be walking in his sleep.

For a moment Poil de Carotte holds back from speaking. He is afraid that his secret joy and the hand he has seized and is almost forcibly holding will vanish.

Then he clenches his fist, shakes it at the village that is dropping off to sleep in the darkness, and cries out:

"Wicked woman! See what you've done. I hate you."

"Hush," says Monsieur Lepic. "She's your mother after all."

"Oh," replies Poil de Carotte, again his simple, cautious self. "I'm not talking this way because she's my mother."

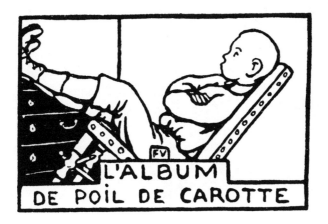

POIL DE CAROTTE'S ALBUM

I

WHEN A STRANGER leafs through the Lepic photograph album, he is invariably surprised. He sees sister Ernestine and big brother Felix in various poses, standing, sitting, well dressed or half dressed, merry or morose, in sumptuous settings.

"And Poil de Carotte?"

"I had some pictures of him when he was very little," says Madame Lepic, "but he was so pretty people kept taking them, and I couldn't manage to keep a single one.

The truth is that no one ever *snaps* Poil de Carotte.

II

He is called Poil de Carotte so persistently that the members of his family hesitate when asked his real name.

"Why do you call him Poil de Carotte? Because of his red hair?"

"His soul is even redder than hell-fire," says Madame Lepic.

III

Other distinguishing marks.

Poil de Carotte's face doesn't exactly argue in his favor.

Poil de Carotte has a nose like a molehill, with two cavernous holes.

Regardless of the quantities removed, Poil de Carotte always has sludge in his ears.

Poil de Carotte sucks snow and lets it melt on his tongue.

Poil de Carotte is a dawdler, and his gait is so slovenly that he could easily be mistaken for a hunchback.

Poil de Carotte's neck is so coated with blue grime that he seems to be wearing a dog collar.

Poil de Carotte has a strange smell, which bears no resemblance to attar of roses.

IV

He gets up first, at the same time as the maid. On winter mornings he jumps out of bed before daybreak and looks at the clock by touch, passing his fingertips over the hands.

When the coffee and chocolate are ready, he breakfasts on the run, taking a bite of anything he can lay hands on.

V

When he is introduced to someone, he turns his head, extends his hand behind him, assumes a look of extreme boredom, crouches, and backs into the wall.

And if he is asked: "Won't you kiss me, Poil de Carotte?"— he replies: "Oh, why bother?"

VI

MADAME LEPIC

Poil de Carotte. Kindly answer when you're spoken to.

POIL DE CAROTTE

Yef, baba.

MADAME LEPIC

I believe I've told you that children should never talk with their mouths full.

VII

He can't help putting his hands in his pockets. And quickly as he may remove them at the approach of Madame Lepic, he's never quite quick enough. One fine day she sews up his pockets with his hands in them.

VIII

Godfather is giving Poil de Carotte a friendly talking to. "You shouldn't lie," he says. "In addition to being ugly, it's useless, because everything comes out in the end."

"That's so," says Poil de Carotte, "but you gain time."

IX

Big brother Felix has just graduated from school, by the skin of his teeth.

He stretches and sighs with contentment.

"What are your inclinations?" Monsieur Lepic asks him. "The decisions you make now will affect your whole life. What do you mean to do?"

"Do?!" says big brother Felix. "Again!!"

X

They are playing parlor games.

Mademoiselle Berthe has been chosen to be "it."

"Because she has blue eyes," says Poil de Carotte.

"How sweet! How gallant! How poetic!" the others cry.

"Oh," says Poil de Carotte, "I've never even looked at them. I only said that to be saying something. It's a conventional remark, a rhetorical figure."

XI

When it comes to snowball fights, Poil de Carotte is a one-man army. He is feared far and wide, because he puts stones in his snowballs.

He aims at the head: to get it over with.

When the pond freezes over and the others go sliding, he arranges a special slide of his own to one side of the ice—on the grass.

At leapfrog, he prefers to be bottom man once and for all.

At prisoner's base, he is indifferent to his freedom and lets anyone who wants to capture him.

And at hide-and-seek, he hides so well that the others forget all about him.

XII

The children compare their heights.

Big brother Felix is a head taller than the others; that can be seen at a glance. But Poil de Carotte and Ernestine have to stand side by side, even if she is a mere girl. And while sister Ernestine stands up on tiptoes, Poil de Carotte, who doesn't like to make anyone feel badly, cheats. He bends his knees imperceptibly to make the negligible difference a little less negligible.

XIII

Poil de Carotte gives Agathe, the maid, a piece of advice:

"If you want to get in good with Madame Lepic, just say mean things about me."

But there are limits.

Madame Lepic doesn't let anyone else lay hands on Poil de Carotte.

One day when a neighbor woman has the audacity to threaten him, Madame Lepic comes running, gives the neighbor a piece of her mind, and rescues her son.

Poil de Carotte is radiant with gratitude. "And now," says Madame Lepic, "you're going to hear from me."

XIV

"What does 'Wheedle' mean?" Poil de Carotte asks little Pierre, whose mother spoils him.

And once he has more or less caught the idea, he cries out, "What I'd like is to eat French-fried potatoes off the platter with my fingers, and to suck a peach right off the pit."

And then after a moment's reflection: "If Madame Lepic loved me so much she wanted to eat me alive, she'd start with my nose."

XV

Sometimes when sister Ernestine and big brother Felix are sick of playing, they don't mind lending Poil de Carotte their toys. With this small share in their happiness, he modestly composes a little happiness of his own.

And for fear that they will want their toys back, he is careful not to appear to be enjoying himself too much.

XVI

POIL DE CAROTTE

Then you don't think my ears are too long?

MATHILDE

I think they're peculiar. Can I borrow them? I'd like to put in sand and make mud pies.

POIL DE CAROTTE

If you'd wait for Mama to warm them, you could bake your mud pies.

XVII

"Stand still a minute. Kindly let me hear that again. So you love your father more than me?" says Madame Lepic from time to time.

And Poil de Carotte's inner voice replies:

"I'm not moving, I'm not saying a thing, and I swear that I don't love either of you any more than the other."

XVIII

MADAME LEPIC

What are you doing, Poil de Carotte?

POIL DE CAROTTE

I don't know, Mama.

MADAME LEPIC

That means you're up to some foolishness again. Do you do it on purpose?

POIL DE CAROTTE

That would be all I need.

XIX

Flattered because he thinks his mother is smiling at him, Poil de Carotte smiles back.

But abruptly Madame Lepic, who was only smiling vaguely to herself, puts on her black wooden face with the black shoe-button eyes.

And Poil de Carotte wants to drop through the floor.

XX

"Poil de Carotte," says Madame Lepic. "Will you kindly laugh politely and without making all that noise?"

"Don't cry," she says "unless you know what you're crying about."

And she also says, "What will ever become of me! He doesn't let out a whimper anymore when I box his ears."

XXI

More of her sayings:

"If there's a spot in the air or a turd on the road, it's headed his way."

"Once he's taken a notion into his head, wild horses won't kick it out of him."

"He's so vain he'd commit suicide to attract attention."

XXII

One day, to be sure, Poil de Carotte does try to commit suicide in a pail of fresh water. He is heroically keeping his nose and mouth under when a cuff upsets the water over his shoes and brings him back to life.

XXIII

Sometimes Madame Lepic says of Poil de Carotte: "He's like me, without malice, more stupid than bad, and too lazy to invent gunpowder."

And sometimes she acknowledges that if the little pigs don't eat him first he'll make his mark later on.

XXIV

"If ever they give me a wooden horse like Felix's for New Year's," Poil de Carotte dreams, "I'll ride away, and I'll never come back."

XXV

To prove to himself that he doesn't care, Poil de Carotte often whistles when out of doors. But the sight of Madame Lepic coming his way cuts his whistling short. It's as painful as if she had broken a penny whistle between his teeth.

There's no denying though, that when he has the hiccups she can stop them by merely appearing on the scene.

XXVI

He is the post office between his father and his mother. Monsieur Lepic says, "Poil de Carotte, there's a button missing on this shirt."

Poil de Carotte brings the shirt to Madame Lepic, who says, "Do you think I need orders from you, you little baboon?" But she takes needle and thread, and sews on the button.

XXVII

"If your father weren't here," cries Madame Lepic, "you'd have done me in long ago, plunged this knife into my heart, and sent me to the poorhouse."

XXVIII

"Can't you wipe your nose?" Madame Lepic keeps saying.

Indefatigably Poil de Carotte wipes his nose on the hem side. When he makes a mistake, he turns the handkerchief over.

When he has a cold, it is true, Madame Lepic rubs him with candle tallow, so thoroughly as to make sister Ernestine and big brother Felix jealous. But she adds, especially for him:

"It's more of a blessing than a curse. It clears the head."

XXIX

After Monsieur Lepic has been teasing him all day, this enormity escapes Poil de Carotte: "You imbecile, can't you leave me alone?"

Instantly he has the feeling that the air has frozen around him and that his eyes are two burning pools.

He stammers, ready to disappear into the ground at a sign.

Monsieur Lepic gives him a long look, but no sign.

XXX

Sister Ernestine is soon to be married. And Madame Lepic permits her to go out walking with her fiancé under Poil de Carotte's chaperonage.

"You go ahead," says sister Ernestine. "Run and jump."

Poil de Carotte goes ahead. He tries hard to run and jump; he gambols in circles like a puppy. But when he slows down by mistake, he can't help hearing furtive kisses.

He coughs.

This kind of thing exasperates him. Suddenly, after baring his head at the village cross, he throws his cap on the ground, stamps on it, and cries out, "Nobody will ever love me, never!"

At that moment, Madame Lepic, who isn't hard of hearing, appears behind the wall, a terrible smile on her lips.

In desperation Poil de Carotte adds:

"Except Mama."

ABOUT THE AUTHOR

Born in Châlons-du-Maine, France, in 1864, JULES RENARD was a poet, novelist, playwright, a member of the Académie Goncourt, and the mayor of the town of Chitry. His most famous works include the novel *L'Écornifleur* (The Sponger, 1892), *Histoires naturelles* (Nature Stories, 1894), and his *Journal* (published posthumously, in 1925). Renard's 1900 stage version of *Poil de Carotte* was a tremendous popular success, and the book has been adapted numerous times for the screen. Renard died in 1910.

ABOUT THE TRANSLATOR

RALPH MANHEIM (1907–1992) was one of the 20th century's greatest literary translators from French and German. After graduating from Harvard, he studied abroad in Germany and Austria. His work includes translations of Brecht, Céline, Günter Grass, Peter Handke, Heidegger, Hesse, and Novalis, among many others. Manheim was the recipient of numerous honors, including the National Book Award and a MacArthur Fellowship.

ABOUT THE ILLUSTRATOR

Born in Lausanne, Switzerland, in 1865, FÉLIX EDOUARD VALLOTTON moved to Paris at the age of seventeen to study art at the Académie Julian. While his portraiture and scenes of middle-class French life received increasing acclaim over the next several decades, he was perhaps most influential for his part in the late-19th-century revitalization of the relief print in Europe. Fascinated by Japanese woodblock printing, Vallotton developed a style notable for what the historian Nathalia Brodskaïa describes as a "candidly flat approach to the plate." Ultimately, he produced an innovative series of starkly composed and provocatively "cool" renderings of passions both public and private, prints in which, Brodskaïa writes, "black and white had lost the sense of representing only light and shade in nature, and had become elements in the stylized language of engraving." Vallotton died in Paris in 1925.

A NOTE ON THE TYPE

POIL DE CAROTTE *has been set in Darden Studio's Corundum Text, a family of types derived from the work of Pierre-Simon Fournier* le jeune. *Fournier's achievement as a typographer is best known in the form of Monotype's interpretation of the "Saint Augustin Ordinaire" types shown in his 1725* Manuel Typographique. *Cut under Stanley Morison's direction in 1925–26, the Monotype version – christened "Fournier" – was under development at the same time as a somewhat darker type that would eventually be given the name Barbou in honor of the publisher of Fournier's* Traité historique sur l'origine et les progrès des caractères de font pour l'impression de la musique *(1765), which provided Morison's models for the types. Morison would have preferred to release Barbou to the printing trade, but a misunderstanding during his absence from the works led to the release of Fournier. But for a handful of appearances, Barbou largely disappeared from view. The present version of the type captures the rich color of the eighteenth-century original and maintains its lively spirit, especially in the italics.*

DESIGN & COMPOSITION BY CARL W. SCARBROUGH